Empty Calories

Kyle Washington

D1522579

Copyright

Contents

Dedication

To DaDa and NeNe

Acknowledgment

Thank you, Kelly Jr., Effie, Thalia, and Roy

Empty Calories

Plural noun

Definition of *empty calories*

: calories from ~~food~~ *relationships* that supply energy but have little or no nutritional value

Prologue

The wind blew harshly, and the tree swung from side to side, unable to control the pressure. Dark and thunderous clouds blanketed the sky, hiding the beautiful bright sun.

The Peak Family had been observing the change in the atmosphere; they wanted to enjoy a simple family picnic in their parents' backyard, but the wind was not allowing them to do so. Some of the family wanted to be there while the rest didn't.

"Ugh! What's with the wind? The weather report said the weather would be lovely! So why is this happening today?" Ellie grunted.

"Don't worry, Mother. The weather will be better in an hour or so. In the meantime, why don't we have some snacks in the house?" Haley suggested.

"Good idea! I'm starving!" Trinity shouted eagerly.

"Alright, come on, everyone, let's get inside. We're having a mini snack party right now!"

The kids jumped, hearing Haley's voice.

Ellie shook her head at her family's childishness and glanced one last time at the cloud.

I hope it goes by quickly, she thought bitterly. If only Ellie knew of the coming storm about to affect her family's lives.

Chapter 1 – Election Night

Frantically pacing back and forth across the largest expanse of the suite of the election night campaign's headquarters, which was in a downtown hotel, Ellie was worried. The atmosphere in the air could cut ice.

Although Dean's three jumpy boys had somehow managed to keep a calming wave steady among the peaking chaos, Ellie Peak was still not convinced she'd win this election this time around. She was already not in favor of her son bringing along his entire family to the campaign headquarters watch party, given the nerve-wracking circumstances.

She thought to herself, *he's a highly paid surgeon; why did he bring these damn kids! I cannot believe I gave birth to Dean. What was I even thinking?*

Apparently, to him, his children could not be left alone at home— something Ellie could never fathom as a mother of five. She was a different kind of a parent. What made her conscience remotely distracted from the running children was the presence of her four other children and their respective families, all under a single roof. They were all there; the election watch party suite was luckily extensive enough to contain this large crowd.

Downstairs, her supporters were waiting and watching the election results in the hotel's ballroom. With her fourth term in office on the line, Ellie had already questioned herself a significant number of times as to why she called them all to join her on this, the most important day in her life.

In her mind, the day could have easily passed with their absence.

Why did I bother? Why did I listen to my campaign manager, who seldom gives me good advice? Stupid Albert!

Ellie had used all sorts of beyond-usual profanity in her head to satisfy her agitation. Just when her thoughts were bumping against her already aching head, an abrupt knock on the double-hinged door caught her off guard.

"Who is it now!" Ellie's loud voice at least made the children stop running. "Can't they see how stressed I am? Why are they all burdening me?"

"I'll take care of it, Mom." Trinity quickly got up from his designated chair, where he was sitting next to the latest woman he was dating, to answer the door for his mother.

Ellie didn't even bother to learn this latest girlfriend's name. Being the eldest of all Ellie's sons, Trinity had a way with his mother. He knew how to be around her, unlike most of the family. Maybe it was because of the similarities of their personalities—domineering, reserved, and deceptive. Or maybe it was because he knew she approved of him. Trinity got that much-needed validation all of Ellie's children wished they received from her. It was no secret she had her favorites in this family.

"Yes, Albert?" he asked. Soaked in utter annoyance as much as his mother, Trinity was displeased to see her campaign manager at the door again. "What do you want now?"

"My apologies," Albert said, as sarcastically as he could, "there's a matter I need to discuss with Senator Peak."

Albert's words were soothing in tone but piercing in meaning. His dual personality was understandable and inexplicable to everyone. They wondered why Ellie got along with the 40-year-old overly diligent man.

"I am afraid it'll have to wait; she's really occupied right now, as you can imagine." Trinity made sure his words were as clear as his cruel intentions.

"It is related to . . . may I please speak to her?" Albert answered in a crisp, clear voice, never giving away too much. He was more loyal to her than anyone in the family.

"What did I say about you not coming in?" Trinity was cut off right in the middle of his sentence by Haley, the oldest of the five siblings. Lightly putting her hand on his brother's shoulder, Haley's eye gestured to him to let her handle this. She didn't want more drama than was already there.

"Yes, you may speak to Mom, but only if you come back in ten minutes." Haley was as smooth as her moves. Being the executive vice president of a Fortune 500 company, Haley had learned how to handle people and get them to do whatever she wanted.

With that, Albert left, leaving behind a smile at the oldest child.

"I have no idea why you put up with him, Mother. He's up to no good! Can you please get a new manager? I don't know why, but he gets on my nerves whenever I look at him." Trinity said

Trinity took back his allotted seat, which was a few feet away from where Ellie was sitting, her eyes never moving away from the giant television screen, and her fidgeting hands supporting her anxiously set poker face. It was a rare sight to see a strong woman like Ellie looking stressed and nervous. She'd never lost an election, but, for some reason, this one was very different.

Ellie's usual overconfident, arrogant, and self-centered self was commonly seen ordering people around and scolding those who did not do things exactly the way she wanted. Being elected for a fourth term only added to her authoritarian personality, but the results were yet to be announced. Ellie's destiny was to be unfurled in front of the entire world.

"With what?" she asked her son, without a hint of interest and intrigue.

"Never mind." Trinity gave up as Haley rolled her eyes at him, his gaze on the screen again just to match his favorite parent.

"No, what were you talking about?"

"It's okay, Mother; we can talk about it some other day in your free time."

Ellie looked at him for a moment, gauging his reaction, trying to see if there was any hidden meaning behind it. When she found none, she freed him from her gaze and turned toward the television.

Apart from Haley and Trinity, there was another preferred child of Ellie, whom she adored the most: Jonathan. Jonathan was the youngest of the family, the most hopeful of all her children. Ellie loved him to death; to her, Jonathan was her exact replica—not only in words but also in manners and personality. She knew if anyone was going to become like her, it would be Jonathan, and, for that, she favored him.

Ellie's husband, Lee, was not fond of Jonathan. It might be because he was the youngest and had been allowed to get away with anything he wanted—in public or private. Over time he eventually resemble his mother in traits and attributes. Lee just never grew close to Jonathan. Where the other children had some of Lee's physical features, Jonathan did not.

Being pampered and constantly taken care of had made Jonathan a brat, even as an adult. Demanding everything all the time, it became usual for him to make unreasonable requests. And, most of the time, he got his way.

"I'm sorry I'm late. Hello, Mother." Jonathan as always made quite an entrance. Being his usual perky self, he came directly to hug his mother in her seat, not caring to meet anyone else on the way.

"How are you, dear?"

"I'm good, Mom. How are you?"

"I'm well, now that you're here, darling."

Jonathan smiled.

Ellie's face instantaneously changed her eyes slightly beaming, seeing her youngest child in front of her eyes. She didn't even notice he was late. Of course, he would be late; no one could possibly say anything to him or see his lack of punctuality as a problem. Jonathan was always calculating and knew how to work a room. Even his wife and children put him on a pedestal.

"It's good that you're here. Waiting for these election results always makes me so anxious," Ellie said.

"Don't worry, Mom. We all believe you'll win; you always do!"

"Thank you so much, my darling."

Ellie was reassured by Jonathan's soothing and compelling voice. That's why she loved him so much; he always knew how and when to quiet down her tension and anxiety. It wasn't a secret; out of all of them, she loved Jonathan the most. She also felt guilty because when Jonathan was young he was molested, and Ellie covered up the crime.

"Where's Suzanne and the kids?" she asked Jonathan.

"We ran into a relative of Suzanne, that's why we were late. She must be coming here soon with the kids."

"Alright."

It was Nancy who spoke now. "Why are we even here? What was the purpose of us here? The latest polls have you losing this election by five points! What's the meaning of this? I can't understand this shit anymore!"

Nancy was the second daughter, yet the most neglected one out of all the children—the only person who understood her was Dean. He was one of the sons, but the second child after Nancy, who Ellie didn't treat with high regard; in fact, she didn't treat them the same way she treated her other children. Everybody in the family knew this bias but just accepted it for what it was. There was nothing wrong with this pair of siblings, except that their personalities didn't coincide with Ellie's. Unlike

Trinity, Haley, and Jonathan, they didn't suck up to their mother as most people did who met Ellie.

As a young child, Nancy couldn't understand why she was treated differently. She would often get into fights and stay out of the house most of the time and didn't bond with her mother. In contrast, Dean was the family clown. While everyone else loved him and enjoyed his sense of humor, Ellie did not. For her, he needed to be as mature, calm, collected, and serious as Trinity and Jonathan.

She once even said, "Why do you try to act so funny? This attitude will take you nowhere but to a circus house."

And again: "This type of behavior isn't good on a doctor! Do you know how many people would laugh at you? If you don't care about your image, please do care about mine!"

It was that day that Dean decided never to be serious again in his life, at least not for the sake of his mother.

"I'm not sure I invited you! Who told you to come?" Ellie snapped directly at Nancy, making sure she knew how she felt about her and her comment. "I don't think anybody here forced you to come. Nobody needs your presence here; go wherever you want!"

That insufferable woman! She thought. *How could she blame me for everything!*

Ellie's nature was like that; even during the most intense of times, she didn't hesitate or hold back to make her daughter feel left out among the rest. At times, Nancy wondered why she still saw her when she didn't want her around. She had enough of her mother's attitude.

Noticing the sudden change of atmosphere, from intense to discomfort, Haley decided to play the oldest of all cards and brought everyone in the suite together. She was the one who knew how to get it right, even at the wrong times and she knew what to do in a time like this and how to make everyone happy and welcoming. She always made it her mission not to upset anyone. Haley had a vibrant, friendly nature; she was friends with not only her little sister but her two sisters-in-law as well.

The wives, the children, and the siblings sluggishly walked toward the expanse of the lounge, adjusting themselves into their comfortable spots, some near Ellie, some too far, as per their ease. The lit television screen was all that the Peak Family stared at.

"The time has come . . . it is when things will be decided, the fourth time for Ellie Peak in office . . . where would it take her and what is her future. We're trying to get ahold of her. As soon as we do, we'll take you to her live . . . ."

"Hold of her?" Ellie suddenly looked at everybody, her body twisting in both confusion and frustration. "What are they talking about? What do they mean they can't get hold of her?"

Everyone remained silent.

"Answer me!"

And with that, everybody knew what was going to happen next.

"Mother, the media and press have been calling like crazy; we didn't think it was the right time for you—"

Trinity was cut off by Ellie. "Where's Albert? Albert! Albert! Albert!"

The nonstop ear-piercing shrieks made Albert, who was outside the suite's door, come into the room. You could tell he knew Ellie was very upset; he'd seen her this way before.

"Yes, ma'am," he answered in both fear and in the hope of mercy. "You called for me."

"Look up! Why was I not informed about the media calling me? Where the hell were you? Did you fall asleep out there when you should be taking care of things in here!"

Ellie's face was flushed, reddening more and more with each passing second. Her feet were stampeding, nothing getting in her way as she marched across the suite toward the window.

"I did come to inform you that the media wanted to interview you, but I wasn't allowed inside."

Albert simply stated the truth, never meeting eyes with Trinity, who was now alert and on his feet, ready to defend himself.

"You should've mentioned what it was about! Don't you know how important this is for mother?"

"But, sir, I—"

"What, sir, huh? Did you not understand how sensitive this is for mother?"

"I . . . I'm sorry, sir."

And just like that, Trinity turned the whole plate around, guns blazing toward the wounded campaign manager.

Ellie was shaking with anger, and everyone in the room had seen this side of her countless times before. Her anxiety was peaking, with only 15 minutes remaining until the election results came in. The recent incident made everything worse for her and her patience. Being calm since the morning, it was the time of day for her. The overwhelming crowd around her and the children running and making noise was the last smidge of disaster she needed to see just before the race was called.

"I don't understand why you people act so immature! You know what it means to me and the hard work I put in, yet you all have no regard, no concern for it!"

Lee walked over and tried to comfort her, but Ellie pushed him away. Lee was always attentive to her, even though, years ago, he suspected Ellie of cheating in their marriage. Ellie was his first and only love; he'd never been with another woman.

"How will I ever teach this family anything!" she said in such a tone that the family knew what was coming next. "I'm sick and tired of hovering over and trying to make you learn things, but, no, you all disappoint me again and again and again . . . you all would be lost without me! None of you know how to make decisions or think for yourselves!"

13

"Get out . . . get out, everybody!"

Ellie gave her final call by snapping her fingers, but nobody moved—not even Albert—who'd by now melted into a sea of shame and guilt.

"Are you all deaf too now? I said out!"

"Get out of this room!" Ellie's shrieks emptied the room, but it still didn't help her calm down. In fact, she was even more frantic now. Her body was shivering more than before, and her pores were exceedingly sweating.

Quickly taking her seat, she was now almost lying in the chair, her head tilted to the side. She could remember taking deep breaths, as they always soothed and calmed her down. She would always do this during stressful times, but, right now, even that wasn't working. Changing her position and now sitting up straight, Ellie's hand was now pressing her left elbow. It hurt. The more she tried to rub her left arm, the worse it hurt with the pain going above her chest.

Still staring at the TV screen, she knew it was only five minutes until the polls closed. She was just waiting for these five minutes to pass so she could go out and get a drink, but the pain was making it impossible

14

to focus. It was unbearable, even for a minute more. All she could think about was how hard this election was this time and how her popularity had gone down in recent years. If she lost this election, how could she face her family, friends, or the public.

A few moments later, there were three soft knocks on the door. When nobody answered or screamed, Albert allowed himself inside, holding a coffee mug that said "Ellie is the best." Jonathan had given her that coffee mug on her last election.

Three seconds in the suite seeing her on the floor, Albert dropped the mug from his hands with a loud thud, pieces of glass going everywhere. As fast as he could, he sprinted across the room, but a massive part of him knew he was too late. Ellie was lying on the floor in front of her designated seat, her hand on her chest and eyes wide open and lifeless. She was pale but still looked strong and in control. Checking her right wrist for a pulse, her most loyal friend knew she most likely had a heart attack.

Just as he turned his head to scream for help, his eyes flickered up at the lit TV screen that had the words, "Ellie Peak has won her fourth term as a US senator" flashing.

Albert smiled seeing the news she won.

Chapter 2 – Lying in State

Although it seemed Ellie mentally and verbally abused her family at times to outsiders, her husband and children all loved and adored her in their own way. It was as if they worshipped the ground, she walked on even though she treated them all so differently. Three weeks after her death, Senator Ellie Peak was lying in state at the US capital as the country and the world mourned the sudden death of the US senator. The massive crowd streamed through the US Capitol Rotunda; every member of Congress and the president needed to be present on this day. But Lee had had enough—enough of being a practical person in public. He already felt like he was tired of people and their bullshit, and he would never fit in, but, this very day, all limits were crossed.

Lee escaped to the restroom to find a moment of peace. He could sense his feelings getting mixed with his thoughts. It rarely happened; he mostly had a clear mind, where he could always divorce his practical notions from his emotions. Being a successful attorney, he learned a long time ago how to separate these feelings. But, today, he wanted to cry.

But why?

Why am I this depressed?

Why do I feel this way?

We were never a happy couple!

Ellie was never nice to him, except in the beginning, when they met at the law firm, they both worked at shortly after graduating from law school. However, this was not the reason Lee rushed to the restroom—it was a comment by a very rude congressman. Despite what day it was and the presence of his relatives, friends, and almost everyone from the political industry, the man unapologetically found Lee in a secluded corner and decided to ask him if he'd start dating again. Lee's mouth hung open at the absurd question, as he stared at him in utter disbelief. He walked away in silence, not looking back even when the Congressman called out his name to stop him—maybe to apologize—but who knew.

Standing alone in the restroom, it appeared to be gloomy and comforting at the same time. Ellie and Lee never had a chatty relationship; they mostly talked about work and their five children, or mostly, three out of five—Trinity, Haley, and Jonathan. Those three were Ellie's only concern; she paid no real attention to what went on in Nancy and Dean's lives, but she made sure they brought honor to the Peak Family name by acting well in public. When it came to Nancy and Dean, Lee had given up

17

on trying to get Ellie to act differently toward them. There was no use telling her anything about them.

Looking in the mirror, Lee thought about their life together, how she would just shout at him, accuse him of having no financial stability even though, as a high-powered corporate attorney he earned millions of dollars. She would tell him that, if it wasn't for her, Lee would never be the man he is today. Unfortunately for Lee, he knew that was true. Their fights would go to the extent where Ellie told Lee he was too "clingy" and "too dependent." Although Ellie treated him that way, Lee could never leave her. He loved her more than anyone or anything. After all, she was his first and only love.

Silently standing there, Lee thought about the early days of their marriage. He suddenly glanced over at a photo on the restroom wall; the photo reminded him of the time he took her to Paris. She looked beautiful on that trip, especially when she was smiling. He often told her that, but she never responded to it. Ellie was a workaholic at that time; he smiled because he remembered that she even worked on their honeymoon. Looking at the photo, his eyes craved to tear up, but they couldn't.

Why? Why can't I cry? Why wouldn't the tears flow?

I wish I had an answer to this!

Lee had thought that for the hundredth time, never getting an answer. The photo made him remember their worst fight. It was the dinner on Jonathan's birthday—and the reason why they fought. Their lack of compassion and intimacy, Lee knew that Ellie was involved with someone else before. As a result, Lee knew Jonathan was not his child. There were shrieks when he taunted Ellie about their youngest child. Her reply made him shut off and spend the night in another room as usual. Ellie would never admit to an affair, but, deep down, Lee knew Jonathan was not his son, and Ellie knew Lee knew the truth.

At that moment, Lee jerked himself away from his thoughts; he looked at himself in the mirror to fix whatever he could and appear presentable and unbroken in front of the thousands of supporters. He had to go out and face them again, acting strong.

Hopefully, this time nobody else will ask me if I'm going to date again. Lee thought.

Haley

Sitting in her seat next to her husband Ross and staring at her mother's coffin, for the first time, Haley was considering quitting her high-powered, high-paying executive vice president career. Never in her life had she thought this day would come. She loved her job more than anything and anyone in the world. Well, of course, not more than her mother.

Why am I even thinking about this, on this day? At this moment? Haley's heart was broken. She'd spent hours in her bedroom since the day her beloved mom died, sobbing in pain and agony. Weeks had passed, but her pain was not subsiding. She was, in fact, wondering if she'd ever get past this, hence the thought of quitting. She was happy in her marriage and felt she had an amazing life, but this sudden loss made her feel lost. For some reason, she found someone in her husband Ross that understood her. Ross understood her preference for work and her mother's role in her life. Having a similar personality, Haley was quite close to Ellie.

Ever since she was a little girl, she spent most of her time with her mother, shadowing all that she did, even at the law office. She could still vividly remember how her mom let her sit in her office chair and she beamed in delight. It was then that she decided she'd become just like Ellie. And she did! But now her mom was gone. Haley, for the first time, was truly lost. Escaping the ceremony that was about to happen, she went outside. She walked to the backside of the capital, ready to smoke as much as she could. Even though she was trying to quit, she needed to smoke now. She only had a pack on her at that time.

Swiftly finding a spot where no one could find her—not even Ross—Haley slipped down against the wall on the dirty ground. The smoke around her was comforting as always. Finding herself lost in her thoughts about her mom and how she was so important for her own wellness, Haley could sense her body shaking before she began crying. She was silently crying, never realizing there was someone looking at her.

"Who the fuck is there?" Haley wanted to keep her voice low, but the unknown presence made her almost jump in fright and shock.

When no answer came from the other end, Haley stood up to walk up to the shadow.

"Are you fucking following me? Who the hell are you?"

Haley was her usual self—upfront and straightforward. Her voice was shaky from crying and all the excessive smoke.

"No, no. I just came here to smoke. Just like you."

The voice was calm, despite Haley's sudden outburst.

Relapsing back in her spot, Haley almost didn't care. The man in front of her was a stranger she'd never seen before. He was probably in his late 20s but looked harmless.

Tugging on the packet, Haley noticed she'd just puffed up the last of her cigarettes.

"Fuck!"

Throwing the pack away in agitation and anger, she closed her eyes, resting her head against the cemented wall.

"Umm . . . you can have mine." The young man held out his pack to her.

Is he still here? Haley thought to herself. Her mind was not working at all.

"But you have only one. Didn't you come here to smoke too?" Haley asked the innocent-looking man standing inches from her. His hair was wavy; it was as wavey as her nephew's; she couldn't help but notice.

"Yeah, but you need it more than me." The man was persistent and sweet.

Taking the cigarette from him and lighting it up, Haley looked at the young man, who was taking a spot beside her now.

"So you're one of my mother's supporters? What's your name?" she asked.

"I came here with my uncle; he was friends with your mother. Oh, I'm Christian"

Christian shook hands with Haley, who was surprised at how comfortable he was to talk to. She handed the cigarette back to him, which he took, before deciding to give it back.

"We're practically best friends now."

Haley couldn't help but chuckle at the young man's comment.

"You have a nice smile."

At that moment, Haley imagined herself kissing this stranger.

Nancy

Nancy and her husband Adam had been fighting ever since Ellie died. Apparently, Adam had always wanted to detach himself from his mother-in-law and her family, but Nancy had never let him do so. Despite the constant insults she received from her mother, she wanted to have her parents in her life. She wanted to be a daughter; she wanted her daughter to have a grandmother and a family, but her husband never understood her desire.

"What's the matter with you? She disgraced us in front of the entire family, yet you never want to skip any of her dinners or stupid get-togethers. I don't like this. I hate it." Adam was clear about his intentions and feelings, but Nancy, his wife, was adamant not to give up yet.

Nancy was in her early twenties when she married her boyfriend. She had to; Ellie made her become a bride as it was not good for her political reputation to have a pregnant and unmarried daughter. Of course, as absurd as it sounded to her, she had to follow through. Surprisingly, Adam was in love with her and didn't hold back about marrying her. Soon, they were a young, newly married couple with a baby girl. Things went pretty crazy for Nancy at a young age. She always seemed to disagree and would lash out at people. It was common to get a call from the school because she was fighting. Nevertheless, Ellie was always there to get Nancy out of trouble.

The two argued at the capital, and Nancy slapped Adam in the face. In all their years of marriage, Nancy had never hit Adam, but she felt it had to be done. Allowing someone, especially when that someone was her husband, to talk to her the way was not something she could take. Adam was not only unreasonable but out of his lane in her mind. It happened while they were standing outside, receiving the sprawling supporters. Their daughter Brooke looked at Nancy in disbelief at what her mother had done.

"Don't be like your mother!" said Adam, cruel with his words.

Nancy couldn't help but stare at him in anger.

"Seriously, Adam? Do you want to do this right now? We're literally walking to her funeral. Let this go right now or just go out of my sight." Nancy's voice was cutting sharp.

Her back was already hurt from a sports injury when she was young. She played sports during her entire teens. She had severe back issues, and it got worse when she got pregnant with Brooke—not that she minded it. She loved having a family, but it was Adam that was giving her mental torture.

"What did you say? Why should I go away? Because of this stupid ceremony for your mother? This fake show of love? No wonder she fell dead on the . . . ."

That's when Nancy slapped her husband again in the face in front of everyone, including the media. After that, she ran toward the ladies' room, with Brooke following behind her. When she reached the ladies room, she saw Jade, her friend from high school, whom she hadn't seen in years.

Trinity

It was finally a moment of peace. While standing near the entrance of the Rotunda, a lobbyist approached Trinity about an opportunity to get a government contract for his very successful construction company. The lobbyist had been waiting for hours to meet him, but the events of the day would not allow them a moment alone to talk. One after the other, elected officials and supporters kept coming to speak to Trinity. Ellie had so many lobbyists who wanted her time. Trinity had no idea. He already had utmost respect for his mother, but now it was peaking more.

Trinity immediately recognized this as an opportunity for his company. So many people who wanted something from his mother now wanted something from him. But why? He was no politician, or did it even matter to them? He started thinking about his future.

What could happen now?

How can I build a bigger empire?

For Trinity, it was the opportunity of a lifetime. As much as he respected his mother, he felt no real grief nor heartbreak for her. Maybe it was the way he was raised or maybe it was part of his personality, but, unlike the rest, he hadn't cried once since her heart attack. He even saw her lying dead on the floor, but no tears came to his stone-cold eyes.

Trinity told the lobbyist: "Email me the details along with relevant documents as soon as you can. I need to look through them right after this ceremony. I need to get started with this as soon as possible." He was clear with his instructions to the lobbyist. His anxieties were peaking toward the beginning of the ceremony. His heart was unexpectedly racing, and his thoughts were rattling against his head. He had a headache. He began to look at his phone, and it caused his eyes to squint while looking at it, but he couldn't put it back in his pocket. He had things to check—things to discover.

Being close to his mother, from the perspective of business and political favors, Trinity had the responsibility of taking care of the things Ellie left undone, or so he thought.

I'll rule this town!

The thought made him shiver with excitement.

Dean

At the hotel before the ceremony at the capital, Dean was still trying to get himself ready for the day's events.

"Come in." A sudden light knock on the door made Dean get out of his baffling thoughts.

He was in his room for hours, and Albert stopped by to check on him and his family. Focusing on how he must have felt, Dean could feel the room suddenly suffocating him. He had a habit of doing this. As an emotional, friendly, and caring guy, he naturally took all of the miseries and sadness of the world upon himself. If any of his siblings were sad, he would end up thinking about it all night. If any of his friends were in trouble, he would get up at night to reach out to them.

Dean's relentless persona of helping anybody and never being okay with seeing sadness and sorrow made it hard for him to tackle death, especially the death of his mother. She never was really close to him, and everybody in the family knew that, including the servants and the assistants. Dean was a successful surgeon, so he had the mindset that he could fix things—even things like his broken relationship with his mother.

Dean never gave up on his mother and having a relationship with her. He knew she loved him; after all, it was because of Ellie that he got into the medical school of choice. Although Ellie treated him with such disrespect, he figured out a way to be around her, but now that she was gone, Dean wanted to cry. No matter what, she was his mother, and now he felt like there was this massive hole in his life without her.

"I just stopped by to check on you and your family. Did you order breakfast?"

Feeling glad to see Albert, he allowed him in, gesturing him to have a seat.

"Are you okay?" Albert's voice was as calm and composed as he was.

"I'm trying to be, Albert." Dean was trying his best to act like one of his friends, but Albert had always kept his distance, despite being there for Ellie as her campaign manager.

"You don't seem okay. Where are Kathrine and the kids?" Albert asked.

Dean smiled and said, "You know she doesn't like to be called Kathrine!"

"Sorry! Where is Kat and the kids?" Albert said, kind of sarcastically. He then went on and on about the ceremony.

Albert's choice of words made Dean chuckle, even in such challenging circumstances. It was a light one, but the conversation brought a glimmer to his eyes.

"Maybe I should stop talking now," Albert said.

"No. It's okay. You're fine," Dean replied, with a pat on Albert's rigid shoulder. He was evidently awkward. It made Dean chuckle more.

"If you don't mind, can I ask you something?" Albert said.

"Yes," Dean replied, his eyes going back to the hollowness of his mind. He was trying to breathe, but his anxiety was not allowing him to stay comfortable doing that.

"If you want, I can get something to make you feel better and get through this day." Albert's voice was cautious now.

"Nothing will be better for a long while. She's gone, just like that. If only I could have a few more minutes with her. I would have told her I loved her." Dean's eyes were shining with tears.

"But she didn't respect you." Albert presented that as a statement.

Dean chuckled again. He was not surprised at Albert's forwardness.

"I know. But I did, and that's okay. I know we've had our differences, and I know she didn't love me as much as she loved others, but I'm sure there must have been a point where she did. I wish I could tell her goodbye, Albert." With that, Dean started crying, holding his head in his hands, his voice shaking as he spoke.

Uncomfortable yet concerned for him, Albert wanted to help.

"I understand; that's why I have something for you," Albert said.

"What?" Wiping off his tears, Dean was now looking up at him in both curiosity and intrigue. He had no clue what he was talking about.

Out of nowhere, Albert's right hand went into his pocket and he opened his fist in front of Dean.

Albert was offering him Benzodiazepine, a high-potency antidepressant drug (street name Benzo), to calm him down.

Jonathan

"Thank you, Mrs. Stones. Thank you for your kind words."

It was the hundredth time he'd said those words.

Jonathan was an eminent sight during Ellie's ceremony. It was the time. Everybody was dressed in black, looking expressionless yet sneaky, randomly seated around the rotunda that Jonathan had spent hours arranging with Ellie's staff and the congressional delegation. He needed a break.

Yes, he did.

Being the favorite child might come in handy but was never easy. Amid the chaos, Jonathan didn't even have time to visit the restroom. Everybody was coming up to him, talking to him, consoling him first and neglecting the rest of the siblings. He had no idea why.

Do they all know about the disparity in the house? The thought made him frantic because he was getting so much attention. The ceremony was nearly over, and it was time for the youngest son to say a few words about his mother.

"Thank you all for joining my family and me on one of our most difficult days. We feel shattered and heartbroken to bear this loss, but what God has written for us shall come. Saying these words is an honor to me: Ellie Peak was a strong woman, a woman of substance and inspiration. Had she been here, she would have used all the positive and uplifting words to guide me through this. That's how she was—motivated, ready, and always a mentor for all of us. Unfortunately, I never thought I'd be doing the hardest thing of my life without her. As hard as it is, let me start by quoting what she . . . ."

Jonathan was applauded by most of the crowd after his ten-minute-long speech. He suddenly felt like the gathering had become more of a congratulatory event for his wise words than the loss of a strong, political woman. He didn't know what to make of it.

Failing to find his elder brothers, Jonathan gave up.

Where were they? The capital is huge; they could be anywhere.

As many times as he'd been to the capital, he'd never explored it all in one go. Where were his brothers and sisters? Have they been to hurt by the fact that it was only him who the congress members asked to speak at her ceremony that made them upset?

Where is everyone? The thought made Jonathan shudder. He needed to get out. He craved fresh air. The crowd was now getting on his nerves, and so was the fake consolation. He knew people only cared about someone after they were gone.

Finally finding an empty corridor, he frantically hopped inside the offices; he had no idea whose it was. Luckily, though, it was empty. Turning on the lights, he took out his phone, dialing a number in his most recent log.

"Hello, governor!" Jonathan was glad that the governor was quick to answer his phone, even though he was somewhere in the capital.

"Hello, Jonathan! I have something important to tell you!"

"Yes, governor? What is it?"

"I just wanted to say I'm extremely sorry, Jonathan."

"What!? Why are you saying sorry? And what are you even sorry about?"

"Jonathan, the thing is . . . we can't give the senator chair to you. The people are against it!"

"What happened?" Jonathan kept replying, in a low husky voice, unable to fathom what was coming from the other end of the phone call.

"I'm sorry!"

"But you told me in person it was going to be me! Was that a lie?" Jonathan was furious.

Throwing his phone against the wall, he landed on the floor, his head spinning in shock at the governor's sudden revelation. The governor, the person who was meant to decide who to appoint to Ellie's vacant senate seat after her death, had gone back on his word. If Ellie had taught Jonathan anything, it was how to deal with your political enemies.

Chapter 3 – Lee

"Yes!" Lee exclaimed, panting heavily from continuously playing golf. *I did it!* The ball he targeted had successfully entered the hole. Despite his failure, he didn't lose hope, nor did he mind people mocking him. He had a successful career as an attorney, which was worth about five million dollars. Glancing around, he could see the beautiful view of the golf club.

The honey color of the sun was bestowing its blessings on the grass, which, in turn, was dancing in the wind, appreciating the warmth. The intertwining of the rich green color and the fresh warm air made the atmosphere more alluring.

Lee sighed. It had been six months since Ellie left them and he was alone and heartbroken. Everything was going back to how it used to be, but it was still hard for him to fathom her death. It felt like she was here one second, and the other, she was gone.

Lee's children had tried to mend his heart and involve him in different activities but to no avail. There was a void in his heart, a pain that couldn't be seen but had left a deep wound. Ellie's death had taken a toll on him. His love for her was making him depressed. Without Ellie in his life, Lee was drowning himself with work and grief. He loved her dearly, even when she neglected him; to him, Ellie was the only one. Lee often thought that her demise was nothing but a nightmare, that Ellie would appear out of nowhere and everything would be as it used to be. But, alas, it was the truth; his Ellie was gone.

Lee had never thought of anyone besides his wife; his loyalty and love for her were beyond words. He could never cheat on her, nor did he believe anyone could replace her in his heart. Lee was now getting tired of second marriage advice from his peers and colleagues. *Why can't they understand my love for Ellie?* he thought, every time. The house had become quieter and more calming, but there was a hollowness after Ellie's death. Lee knew the house could be revived again, but the hollowness would remain forever.

One day, Lee visited Ellie's grave with a bouquet of Lilies, her favorite. Sitting beside her grave, he cried for hours, pleading to get a glimpse of his dear wife.

"Y . . . you can taunt me all you want, l . . . lo . . . love you. I . . . w . . . will never complain, but do not leave me, please." He requested, wailing, but to no avail; she was never coming back.

I wonder what I need to do to get rid of this pain? Lee thought.

"Hey!" Lee heard a shout in the distance. Not caring much about it, he continued observing his surroundings. "Hey! Lee!" He heard the voice again.

Surprised, Lee turned around to look for who was calling him. The frown on his face upturned in a wide smile when Lee saw who was shouting his name. A man around his own age was striding toward him with a mischievous smile on his face. It was Edward—his best friend and childhood neighbor.

"Hey, bud . . . ." Edward took Lee in his warm embrace, hugging and showing him how much he missed him.

"Hey . . . ." Lee was overwhelmed with emotions.

Pulling back from the hug, Lee could see the sorrow in Edward's eyes. He knew Edward was also feeling his pain.

"I still can't believe it!" Edward said. "She was like a sister to me.

"I know . . . ." Lee expressed his feelings. "I miss those times; they were the best!" He chuckled, with tears in his eyes.

For the next few hours, the long-time friends reminisced.

"I should get going before Mia goes on a rampage," Edward said, glancing at his watch.

"Alright. I should get going too," Lee said, packing up his belongings. The two parted ways with a promise to meet each other soon.

Driving past the street, Lee saw a black car on the side of the road, hood wide open and a woman leaning on it, struggling to find out what was wrong with the engine. He stopped to see if he could help her.

"Hello! Is everything alright?" Lee politely asked the woman.

"Huh?" Startled, the women looked up from the hood. "Oh . . . um . . . yes!" she replied, still puzzled by the sudden action. She was dressed in a white blouse and pencil skirt. With her big hazel eyes and lean body, she was a beautiful woman in her early-30s. Her soft brown curls flowed to her shoulders. This was the first time Lee felt his heart skip a beat, looking at a woman, especially after Ellie's death, but the lady was young enough to be his daughter.

"Okay," Lee replied in a friendly tone, smiling slightly at her nervousness. She stepped aside and let him look into her car.

"Ah . . . ." He paused, deliberating. "The engine overheated. Your hose has come loose; I'll reconnect it for you."

"Oh gosh! Thank you so much," she said.

Lee fixed the problem and closed the hood. Turning toward the young woman, he said, "Your car is now fine; hope it won't trouble you anymore."

"Thank you again!" she said gleefully, "Oh! I'm so sorry, I didn't even introduce myself." With that, the woman sheepishly introduced herself, extending her hand toward Lee. "Hi! I'm Holly."

"I'm Lee." Lee shook her hand and smiled warmly at her.

An awkward silence fell on the two after the brief introduction.

"Uh . . .," he said, uncomfortable, "I think I should get going now."

"Would you like to grab a cup of coffee from a nearby cafe? It'll only take a minute, I promise. Take it as a token of appreciation for your help."

"Okay," Lee said.

*****

While dressing himself up, Lee pondered about the past few weeks; he couldn't quite comprehend how fast things had moved on. *I look good, I guess,* he thought, checking himself in the mirror. He couldn't understand why he was nervous. *What's wrong with me? I'm just going to visit Holly for lunch,* he thought.

Lee and Holly remained in contact, texting and calling each other and getting more comfortable together. In fact, Holly had become medicine for his pain and sorrow; her smile was like a rainbow on a rainy day. Lee was coming back to life, and his colleagues and family could see it. He didn't know what it was—friendship or love—but he did know Holly had become a significant part of his life. He had a soft corner for her, as they were both suffering from the death of their spouses; their pain and anguish were mutual.

Lee arrived at Holly's house around two in the afternoon with a bouquet of roses and a box of her favorite chocolates.

"Hello!" Holly greeted Lee, opening the door to let him step inside. "You're early today; I wasn't expecting you till three."

"Hey!" Lee replied, giving her the chocolates and bouquet. "Yeah, I got free early today so I thought I'd visit you."

"Oh! Thank you so much, Lee! You always know what I want," she said to him.

Lee could only smile and nod; he was delighted to see Holly liked her presents. He roamed around the room while scanning the surroundings.

Holly lived in a small two-bedroom house; there was a kitchen equipped with a dining table next to a living room that contained a leather sofa.

"How do you like my humble abode?" Holly asked Lee, watching him look around the living room.

"It's very well decorated. Did you do everything on your own?" Lee asked.

"Yes! But my colleagues helped me design it," she said excitedly, "the perks of working in an architecture company."

Lee laughed at her naiveté, feeling delighted to know someone like her.

Holly and Lee shifted to the dining area to have their lunch. He tried to help her with setting the table, but she politely declined and pushed him to take a seat on the table.

"I made it myself. I know what you like, so I wanted to impress you!" Holly declared, fetching the plates and cutlery from the cupboards.

"Oh! You didn't have to. I would have eaten anything," he told her, observing her moving back and forth with the dishes.

"No way! I love doing things for you," Holly told Lee while casting a meaningful glance toward him.

Lee shied away from her bold words and gazed at the table, but his cheeks' flushing in embarrassment gave his nervousness away. Holly laughed wholeheartedly at his reaction, teasing him. Their conversation, mixed with laughter, continued on through lunch. Both of them were fixated on each other as if they were in their bubble, not caring about anyone.

"Ah! I'm full!" Lee joked, walking into the living room, making Holly laugh at his antics.

"Would you like to watch a movie?"

"Sure. But please, no cliché ones."

"Alright. Alright." Holly laughed, giving in.

"How about *Breakfast at Tiffany's*?"

"Are you suggesting this movie because I'm much older than you?"

"I don't care about your age; I enjoy your company."

Lee and Holly watched the movie silently, enjoying the calm and soothing environment. Holly brought popcorn, two bottles of Pepsi, a bag of Doritos, and dips. Both of them were so immersed in the movie that they didn't realize when the distance between them became nonexistent. Their shoulders caressed each other, leaving a rush of adrenaline behind. Both of them knew what was going on, but they remained oblivious, stubbornly wanting the other to make a move.

"Lee," she said, moving her body toward him, "I . . . I wanted to tell you something!"

"What?" he asked, nervous and excited, turning toward her.

"Actually . . . ." Holly shifted her eyes back and forth from Lee to the television.

"Em—"

Holly glanced up and interrupted his speech, taking his face in her hands, kissing him hard on the lips, stopping him from uttering anything. Lee was shocked; his eyes went wide and still, but his lips slowly moved with hers. Astonishment washed over him. Their lips complemented each other, as if they were two pieces of a puzzle coming together to solve it.

*****

The couple went on a date the next weekend. Lee knew Holly loved going to festivals and events, so he prepared a festival date. They decided to meet each other near the marble angel fountain located at the heart of the park. Lee arrived half an hour early, excited as a little kid with a new favorite toy. He wore a button-down, light gray collared shirt and black jeans, completing the outfit with white sneakers.

I hope this day goes well; the weather and the ambiance really complement each other, he thought. *I hope Holly says yes to my proposal.*

Gazing around the park, Lee looked at the people enjoying and making memories with their loved ones. Glancing at his watch, he saw it was six in the evening. *Where's Holly? Did she bail on me?* he thought. *Should I call her?*

"Hey!" Lee heard her voice before he could call her. He turned around to face her, and there she was, beautiful and graceful as ever. Clad in a wine-red summer dress, Holly looked breathtaking. His breath stopped for a moment as he stared at her in awe.

"Hel-l-l-o-o-o, Le-e-e?" she called him out.

"Oh, yes!"

"Where did you go?" She joked.

"I think I visited heaven." He teased, playing along.

"Really? What did you see there?"

"An angel."

His reply made Holly blush furiously, making Lee laugh at her innocence. "Come on, let's go and enjoy our date."

The couple rode every ride they could, not caring about the time. They got lost, relishing the fun activities at the festival. The last ride was the couple's favorite—the Ferris Wheel. Holly was a bit scared initially, but Lee persuaded her, promising to protect her at all costs. His words reassured her.

"Wow! I really enjoyed today, Lee!" Holly gushed.

"Thank you; I'm glad you loved it."

"Absolutely! I've never enjoyed myself this much in my whole life. It was the best."

"You look beautiful when you smile."

"Hush! Stop teasing me," she muttered, blushing.

"Seriously, you are!" he declared, sighing.

"I love you, Holly."

"I love you too, Lee."

"Holly, you've made my life whole; there was a void in my heart after Ellie's death, and you completed it, showering me with love and attention. I don't understand how I got so lucky. Holly, you've moved not only my heart but my kids' as well. They love and treat you as if you were a part of the family."

"Lee, I—"

"No, let me say it. I want to tell you everything, pour my heart out to you. I don't want to lose you in any way; you've become a significant part of my life. Holly, I'm deeply in love with you and want to spend the rest of my miserable life with you. Will you please do me the honor of marrying me and stay with me forever?"

Everything stopped—lights, wind, breaths—a silent pause engulfed the air.

"Yes!" Holly yelled, tears in her eyes, "I will marry you, Lee."

Lee put the ring on her finger and embraced her in his arms, wrapping her so tightly, afraid she might disappear into thin air. Leaning back from the hug, Lee kissed Holly's face, her eyes, her nose, her cheeks, her chin, and finally her mouth.

It was a new beginning for them and their love.

*****

47

Two months later, Lee stood at the altar, dressed in a tuxedo; he still looked as handsome as when he was young. Lee couldn't believe it; the day he was eagerly waiting had arrived—his wedding day. He was getting married to Holly; she was finally going to be his wife. He was completely and irrevocably in love with her. Eagerly waiting for his soon-to-be wife, Lee observed his surroundings. His children were there for the wedding, sitting beside their partners. Even Jonathan was there, which was surprising, as the father–son duo did not meet each other's eye.

"Here comes the bride . . .."

The whole church lit up upon Holly's entry; she looked mesmerizing in a white mermaid gown, long net sleeves, and a bunch of Dahlias in her hands. Everyone was in awe of the bride, especially Lee, who was standing stunned at the altar, staring at his beautiful fiancée lovingly.

Lee extended his right hand to Holly when she reached the altar, helping her step up on the stairs. The couple was smiling widely at each other, cherishing the moment of their union.

"Today, we're here to . . .." The wedding procedure passed in a blur. Lee couldn't remember anything, not even the vows, guests, dinner, or the reception. The only thing he could remember was Holly.

*****

Life was blissful for the newly wedded couple; his family also got along with Holly, especially Nancy and Dean. Nancy was happy to know her, and their minds matched each other. Lee was glad to see Holly was embraced by his family and that they loved her. Holly was the type of personality who befriended everyone she met. People just loved her.

As time went by, Lee and Holly's bond grew stronger; anyone who looked at them would envy their love. Lee was proud and fascinated to find such a loving partner in Holly. It wasn't that Lee didn't miss Ellie—he did, but it was bearable now. He could confine her to his good memories.

Lee began to transfer assets to Holly and gave her power of attorney. He wanted to secure a backup plan in case anything went wrong. He showered her with expensive gifts, perfumes, dresses, jewelry . . . whatever she wanted, and pampered her, treating her like a queen. They had been married for only three months, but, to Lee, it was as if he'd known her his entire life. Sure, he had a "family," but it seemed as if Holly became the only one.

Lee's daughter Nancy used to visit them often with a blonde woman, Jade. Trinity busied himself with his business and deals; he barely had time to meet anyone and did not even want to. Haley frequently cancelled her visits, and Lee was worried when she did. Initially, he thought she must have been busy with work, but, the other day, while passing by, Lee saw her in front of a coffee shop with a younger guy. Before he could approach them, they were gone. Otherwise, Dean was still drowning himself in grief, self-medicating with prescription drugs. His health was deteriorating. Lee wished he could do something for him; he tried but failed every time. Lee didn't care or worry about his youngest son, Jonathan; he was not his blood. He struggled with what he knew was the truth about Jonathan not being his son, but no one else knew this secret.

After Ellie's death, his children's lives had changed entirely. On the façade, she was guarding them and making them stable, but Lee knew it was the opposite.

*****

Ring. Ring. Rin—

"Hello?" Holly picked up the phone, which had been ringing for the past fifteen minutes.

"Hello, darling!" a seductive and teasing voice answered. Holly gasped, eyes wide and mouth open.

"What do you want!? Why are you calling me again!" she yelled.

"I was just wondering how my l-o-v-e-l-y baby is doing," the man replied, getting on her nerves, "I missed you. I visited the club, but you weren't there. I want to meet you."

"Are you out of your mind, Chris!? I'm married now! I'm never going to meet you ever again; I left that life a long time ago."

"Oh really?" he sneered, "I think I should let your loving family know how great of an escort you are."

"Shut up!"

"Or what about I tell them that you used to con people." He continued, mocking her, ignoring her pleads. "Once a thief, always a thief!"

"No!"

51

"Huh . . . what do you think your new husband will do?" He laughed at her discomfort.

"Please . . . no . . . no . . . don't do this, Chris. I'll do anything—" She sobbed.

"Seven o'clock at Dear Irving."

"Wait. What—"

"I'll be waiting for you, babe!" He teased and hung up.

Holly was frightened; she didn't know what to do. Chris had been her customer and ex-lover when she worked as an escort. But three years ago, she left that life and severed any kind of contact related to it. Chris was an overprotective and possessive lover, though, and Holly was frustrated by his behavior. However, now that he was back, Holly didn't know what he'd do.

The very next day at the breakfast table, Holly was pondering over whether she should visit Chris when Lee approached her.

"Hey, Holly." Lee kissed her on the lips. "What are you thinking about?"

"Huh . . . nothing," she replied, startled.

"Alright. I have to go to Glen Loch today for a meeting with a client; how about you go with me and we can explore the town afterward?"

"Ah . . . I . . . I must meet a childhood friend today. She's in town currently, and we decided to meet for lunch and shopping."

"Can't it be delayed, babe? This is a one-time opportunity; I was looking forward to this long weekend. I already had planned what we'd be doing there."

"I wanted to, babe. But . . ."

"But?"

"Uh . . . my girlfriends insisted on meeting on that day. They are not available on any other day."

"It would be fun if you could join me."

"I know, babe."

"Oh, alright." Lee sighed, disappointed.

"It's okay, babe; we can visit the town another time," Holly reassured him. "We'll have more days to come where we can go out and have fun. You should go and enjoy without me; I promise I'll make it up to you!"

"Yeah." Lee smiled affectionately at his wife. He loved her so much; his world revolved around her. Lee trusted Holly and felt she would never betray his trust, always staying faithful to him. But alas! Fate had other plans.

At exactly seven o'clock, Holly arrived at the bar. Nervous and frightened to meet Chris again. She spotted him sitting in a corner booth, smoking. Giving herself a pep talk, she approached him. Chris, who was lost in his thoughts, felt a gaze on him and looked upward. Upon seeing Holly in his sights, he gave her a mischievous glance, smirking slightly. Holly stood frozen, knowing she'd entered a lion's den.

"Come on, Cherry. I don't bite!" He mocked, calling her by her stage name. "Yet."

Angry at her foolish decision, she forcefully sat down in front of him. Holly was alert the whole time, anxious and worried about what might happen next. She wanted to convey the message to Chris that she was no longer interested in him and was living a beautiful life with Lee. Holly could only control her heart, but her body had other ideas. It was making her insane.

"Okay, I came here! You got what you wanted!" Holly declared. "I have to go now. Don't ever call me again."

"Aww . . . why do you want to leave so early?" He taunted her, "The night is still young; how about we go somewhere else and discuss more?"

"No!" She rushed out of the bar. Panting, she leaned on the side of the building, trying to grasp the situation. Suddenly, she felt hands on her, one pulling her toward an alleyway and the other hand on her mouth. She was scared for her life. The person pushed her against the building wall and kissed her—hard. Holly knew those lips; she'd kissed them more than she had breathed. It was those soft lips that made her lose control. Opening her eyes, she confirmed her suspicions; it was Chris.

Holly didn't want to betray Lee, but she couldn't resist the attraction she had for Chris. She responded to him eagerly, matching and moving with him. One thing led to another, and the whole meeting turned into a night full of pleasure. Holly thought this would be her last meeting with him—little did she know it would turn into a full-fledged affair. She started to visit him whenever she could, without letting Lee know about anything, making up fake stories to cover her affair.

Over the next six years, Holly manipulated Lee, portraying herself as vulnerable and innocent. Because Lee was fixated on her, he never questioned her and believed whatever she told him. She had him wrapped around her fingers. Gradually, she started stealing his money, transferring it into other accounts. Holly was just waiting for an opportunity, and when she found one . . ..

Chapter 4 – Haley

Driving past her favorite park signboard, Haley turned left on the road and parked her car. She sighed, placing her head on the steering wheel, and shutting her eyes tightly. From the past few days, her thoughts were scattered all over the place, and she couldn't figure out a way to cope with the sudden loss of her mother, Ellie.

Haley was contemplating resigning from the company she'd been working in for years now. After all, it was because of her mother only that she started as an intern there years ago, and now she was the vice president of global sales. *What would Ross and the kids think of this decision?* It had been two years since Ellie died, but the loss was still hard. Her mother was the water to her flowers; without her, she didn't know how to bloom anymore. Haley's life was going downhill with each passing day; it was if she'd lost her peace of mind somewhere. Ross had tried to help her bounce back to her previous dominant self, but that turned out to be fruitless.

Walking along the trail, Haley gazed at the sunset, imagining what her life would be like if Ellie were still alive. The warm wet grass grazed her feet lightly, leaving behind a pleasant feeling. The wind was teasing her, going back and forth, slightly touching her.

Haley felt a presence beside her. Looking from her peripheral vision, she saw a guy standing in the distance. *Why does he look familiar?* She thought. *Have we met before?* Squinting her eyes to get a closer look, she realized it was Christian, the guy she'd met at her mother's funeral. She'd never met anyone as fascinating as him; there was something in him that attracted her to him—the tall, hooded dark brown eyes, wavey black hair, lean but muscular body that looked like an Adonis, there was just something about him, or maybe everything. Christian was wearing a round-neck T-shirt and black shorts, pairing them with white sneakers.

"Hey! You're Christian, right?" she asked.

"Huh?" Christian looked at her. "Oh, yes! I'm Christian." Pausing, he asked, "You're the senator's daughter? Haley, right?"

"Yes. Yes, I am." She half-smiled.

"So . . . umm, what are you doing here. I mean . . . you don't . . . I don't know how to put this . . . you don't appear . . . happy . . . to me." He hesitated.

"What do you mean?" she asked, confused.

"No offense, but you look a bit pale, your eyes have dark circles, and you have sunken cheeks and no glimmer in your eyes. Are you alright?"

Haley was speechless. Ross, who was her husband, was unable to notice these simple things, but this guy, a total stranger, could look into her soul. She was both horrified and amazed. When she saw Christian was waiting for her reply, she dumbfoundedly said in a small voice, "No . . .."

What's wrong with me? Why did I say that? And that too to a stranger? She thought, scolding herself.

"I . . . I don't know what you're going through right now, but I'll do my best to help you overcome it . . . if you want me to."

"Thank you so much." Haley genuinely smiled for the first time since her mother's death.

"Here, keep this card," he said, sticking out his hand to extend his business card to Haley.

"You're a sculptor?" she asked, surprised and still looking at the card information.

"Yes," he said, laughing. "Why do you sound so shocked?"

"I didn't imagine you as one. I mean, I thought you were a businessman."

"No way! My uncle wanted me to work with him, but I was never interested in it. I love making sculptures." Smiling, Christian gazed up.

"Can you make my sculpture?" *The hell, Haley! Where did that come from?*

Surprised, Christian stared at her for a second, then murmured, "Sure. I'd love to!"

There was a twinkle in his eyes, a mischievousness that sent shivers down her spine. *I wonder how it'll go?* The thought excited her.

Clearing her throat, Haley muttered, "I should be going now; my husband is waiting for me."

"Oh! Alright." He paused. "About the appointment . . . is this Sunday good for you?"

"Yes."

"Perfect! See you at six."

Haley nodded. The two went their ways, engrossed in their own thoughts. Sighing, Haley made her way home, where Ross waited for her at dinner.

"Hey, babe!" Ross greeted her, opening the brown wooden gate for her. "How was your day?"

"Hey, honey!" she replied, settling on the loveseat. "It was good."

"That's good to hear." He kissed her affectionately, and leaning back, he murmured, "How are you holding up?"

"It's . . . it's alright, I guess. I never thought I'd get separated from her and still feel this way years later. I miss her a lot."

"I miss her too."

The couple sat, embracing, their pain intertwined with each other.

"Are you hungry? Should we eat now, or do you want to wait?" he asked Haley, leaning back.

"No, no. No need to wait." She reassured him. "Let me just go freshen up, and we can eat then."

Ross had always been loving and compassionate toward her. There wasn't a single time that she doubted her decision to marry him. In fact, Haley found their couple compatible and was content that she married an ideal guy, someone every girl dreamed of.

Haley was blessed; with three great kids and a loving husband, she believed their love would be eternal and that nobody would be able to come between them, but she didn't know fate had other ideas.

*****

Haley was uncertain about what to wear for her appointment; she rummaged through the closet again and again. "Huff," she exhaled. *Why am I this worried? I don't have to impress anyone! Why am I getting so worked up? I wonder what Ross must be doing now.*

Ross had left for camping in the woods with his friends early in the morning. He was reluctant to leave her alone in this state, so Haley had to reassure him again and again that she was alright.

"Okay . . . but if you need anything, and I mean anything, call me ASAP, okay?" he told her, kissing her tenderly on her forehead.

Shaking her head and shaking off her daydreams, she glanced at the wall clock. The hands-on clock let her know that she had an hour to get ready. Frustrated, she started combing her hair and scanned her bedroom; her eyes moved past the jumpsuit that rested on the chair, and she paused. Taken aback, she glanced back at the jumpsuit. Gradually, the frown on her face turned into a wide smile. *This is it!* She thought excitedly.

Dressing up quickly, she observed herself in the mirror to finalize her look. The white, off-shoulder jumpsuit was styled with black wedges and a bag. *Okay, relax! You look beautiful, Haley; no need to get so jumpy. You can do it!* She comforted herself.

Haley fetched the business card from her bag and entered the address in the GPS. She was both excited and nervous about her appointment; it was the first time she was experimenting with something she wanted to do. It took half an hour for her to reach the location, which Haley found astonishing; it meant that Christian lived close by. She observed the location, a two-story, marbled, cream-colored house with a small backyard. She immediately fell in love with the house.

"Are you going to come in, or are you just going to daydream?" A voice whispered in her ear.

Haley turned around, surprised, and found Christian standing at a little distance from her.

"Oh . . . um . . . hi," she sheepishly said, "I didn't see you there."

"I was out grocery shopping." He chuckled. "Let's go inside."

Nodding, she followed him inside the house, gawking at the beautiful interior design. Haley saw a sliding door at the rear that gave a view of the beauitiful backyard garden.

"You're right on time, madam." Christian teased her, glancing at the digital clock on the shelf.

"What can I say? being an executive, a wife, and a mother has taught me time management." She played along, smirking.

Christian laughed and shook his head.

"Shall we start? Or do you want to have dinner first?"

"No, it's okay. I'm going out with my family after the session."

"Oh . . . alright . . . let's start the session then."

Christian guided Haley to the basement, where he'd established a studio. In the middle, there was a stool and a plinth placed in an otherwise empty space; the right and the left side had a built-in shelf on the wall that consisted of all sculpturing equipment and materials.

"Over here!" Christian walked to the stool placed on the right. "Please sit over here."

Tentatively, she made her way to him and placed herself on the stool, shifting every two seconds to get in a comfortable position. Christian walked to the plinth and gathered the equipment.

"I need to have your consent . . . to touch you so I can work on the piece," he asked her, hesitatingly.

"Uh . . . sure!" she replied, anxious.

Christian made his way toward her; her heart started to beat faster in anticipation. Taking a position in front of her, he ran his fingers through her hair, touching every wave. He slid his fingers between her hair, feeling the silky soft texture. Then he slowly stroked her cheeks, eyes, nose, and chin, studying every part of her with care. Gliding his hands onto her neck, he felt its shape, sensing its slow movement when she swallowed tensely.

Moving past her throat, his hands slid down her shoulders, stopping at the curve of the shoulder. Timidly, as if to not scare her, he lightly caressed her collarbone from one end to the other. She gasped and clenched her fist tightly, her lips parting slightly. He moved his hand to her lips, halting it a breath away from her mouth. Entranced, he caressed her lips, feeling the curve of her mouth, watching her take in a shallow breath.

Christian ceased his hand movements, staring intensely at Haley and observing every detail. Haley felt a penetrating gaze on her face but didn't move her eyes from the ground. She was afraid that something might happen if she did.

A second passed. And then two.

Giving in, she glanced up. Their eyes met, and a spark lightened between them. Christian and Haley tried to convey their emotions, listening and conversing with their eyes, twinkling and seducing. No words were spoken; only the heavy breathing could be heard. It wasn't clear who moved forward first; was it Christian? Was it Haley? Or both? Nevertheless, their lips intertwined with each other. What started as a slow sweet kiss turned into a passionate, urgent kiss; their arms embraced each other.

Leaning back from the kiss, he moved to her neck and shoulders, placing butterfly kisses along the way.

"Wait . . . ." She gasped, pushing him back. "I cannot do this! I'm married . . . ." Haley didn't know what she wanted. One second, she wanted him to stop, and the next, she wanted him to keep going. His hand moved toward the zipper on the back of her jumpsuit, and he started unzipping.

Ring. Ring.

The ringtone hit Haley like a bucket of cold water, bringing her back to reality. She pushed Christian away and retrieved her phone from her bag.

"Ross," flashed on the screen of her phone. Looking at her husband's name, she felt goosebumps spread all over her body.

"Are you going to take it?" Christian asked, a breath away from her.

When did he move closer?

Taking her face in his hands, Christian murmured, "You want this as much as I want it. Accept it." He caressed her lips with his. "Don't answer!" Haley felt herself losing; her resolve to fight against this temptation was gone. Christian kissed her, urging her to kiss him back, and she did! Reluctant at first, but then losing herself in him, she ignored the ringing phone in the background.

*****

Something heavy was placed on Haley's waist that was stopping her from moving; she shifted from one side to the other but to no avail. Annoyed, she opened her eyes and blinked at the eminent light rays coming from the window. Haley gauged the room, taking in every detail in her mind until her eyes stopped at Christian. He was sleeping peacefully beside her, with one hand on her waist and the other beside him. She smiled, recalling the ravishing night. It was the best night, but how would she explain to Ross and the kids why she was out all night and didn't answer her phone. Playfully, she inched toward him and pecked Christian on the lips to wake him up.

"What . . .?" he groggily asked, peering at her with one eye.

"Hey!" she cheekily muttered.

Christian gazed at her face and then her body, wrapped in white silk sheets. "You're beautiful."

"I . . . I don't know," she said, blushing. "What time is it?"

"Uh . . . ." He looked beside him; the clock at the nightstand read 9:00 a.m. "It's nine in the morning."

"Shit!" She shot up hurriedly. "I have to be at the office right now!"

Haley's sudden movement caused the sheets to flow down, revealing her naked body to Christian. She shyly tried to hide herself, but the deed was done now. Christian moved her back on the bed and rolled on top of her. The ice melted with the fire. Skin to skin, soul to soul, they become one once again. It was half-past eleven when Haley was finally able to get out of bed and dress, despite Christian's lingering touches.

"Why are you in a rush?" he asked, laying on the bed, watching her put on her clothes.

"Uh . . . I'm giving my resignation today," she told him, sighing.

"Oh! That's a big move. Why are you resigning?"

"It's time for me to move on."

"When will I see you again?"

"Soon." Kissing him, Haley exited from the front door.

Sigh. It was an exhausting day for Haley; the morning hookup, the chaos at the office when she gave her resignation, and the night before left her worn out. The house was tidy when she reached home. *Ross is home*, she thought, *but where is he?*

The sound of the water splashing on he floor could be heard in their master bedroom. The regret and guilt of cheating on her husband burdened her shoulders. Removing her clothes and joining Ross in the shower, she made a vow that she'd never meet Christian again.

. . . except that Haley didn't know she wouldn't be able to keep her promise!

*****

The bed creaked as their entangled bodies moved in sync; panting, groaning, and moaning enveloped the bedroom. The clothes were scattered on the floor, and there was an urgent desperation in the atmosphere.

Christian rolled on his side, panting from the intense lovemaking. He engulfed Haley in a warm hug and kissed her slowly.

"I missed you," he said, going again for a kiss.

"We just saw each other yesterday, Christian." She chuckled, kissing him back.

"Yeah, but I need you every time, every day with me. I don't want to be away from you for even a second." He declared, spooning her.

"I know, babe, but I need to get back to Ross and the kids."

"I don't like him getting near you! Why don't you leave him?" He frowned, a dark expression forming on his face. He asked this same question every time they were together.

"I will; I just need some time. When everything settles down, then I will." She reassured him.

It had been two years since their affair started, and the couple had become more intimate than they were before. Haley had stopped visiting her family since she'd found comfort in Christian. The guilt she initially had for cheating on Ross was now gone. There was a side to Christian that Haley didn't like, but she ignored it: he had a bad temperament. Nonetheless, Haley couldn't resist the passion.

Christian didn't like Haley interacting with Ross; he'd get anxious whenever she was with her husband, or when he'd be calling and texting to check up on her. Haley found his behavior endearing, loving the attention she was getting from him. She needed this type of attention, and Christian gave it to her. Aside from his possessive nature, Christian was a great lover; he understood her like no one ever had. Haley loved him; it made her neglect his obsession with her, but there were times when she herself was unable to overlook it.

Haley knew she was playing with fire, but it gave her a sense of freedom—and a thrill she was longing for; she didn't mind getting burned by it.

"Haley? Babe?" Cristian asked.

"Huh?" Haley turned her face toward him.

"Are you free this weekend?"

"Yes, I am. Why?"

"Let's go out on a date. It's been a month since we went on one."

"Really?" She turned around.

"Really." He kissed her shoulder.

"But . . . wait . . . where are we going?"

"That's for me to know and you to find out!" He teased, shifting her near him, placing her head on his chest and enclosing his arms tightly around her.

The weekend came, and the couple went out on a date. Haley was overjoyed when she saw the date venue. It was the park where they met each other. The park was a miracle for them, a place that allowed them to meet their destiny. The couple walked along the trail, hand in hand, enjoying the moment.

"Hey, do you want something to drink?" he asked her, "I'm thinking of getting a lemonade."

"Oh yeah, bring me one too," she said.

Haley was left alone for ten minutes when a guy approached her.

"Hey!" he said. "Can you please help me with directions?"

"Huh? Sure, what do you want to know?"

"Uh . . . actually I—"

"Who do you think you are? with a death stare on his face, "Why the hell are you flirting with my girl!" Christian punched and kicked the guy. A huge crowd started to form around them.

"Chris! Chris! Christian! Leave him alone." She struggled to pull him back, but he didn't let go and only moved back when the guy's face was unrecognizable.

Christian gripped Haley's wrist and forced her into the car, going around the car to the driver's side. *What the fuck was that!?* she thought. The ride to his house was made in silence; no one dared utter a word. This wasn't the first time it had happened; Christian had been hostile whenever a guy approached Haley. His love for her was twisting into an obsession. Haley was becoming weary of his behavior; initially, she ignored it, but

73

now she wanted to get out of this toxic relationship. She didn't want to be with a person who shadowed her every movement!

"I don't think this is going to work . . . ." She hesitated, walking into the living room. "I think we should end this!"

"What are you talking about, babe?" he asked, encircling his arms around her, his front to her back.

"I mean we should break up!" she said firmly, removing herself from his embrace.

"What?" he muttered, "What are you talking about? You're joking, right?"

Haley didn't utter a word, confirming his suspicion. Christian's whole body burst into flames; he appeared red—enraged and wild. The lightness in his eyes turned dark because he saw Haley's attempt to leave him as a betrayal.

"Oh! You're going to leave me?" He hissed. "Let's see if I'll let you!" he shouted, marching toward her.

"Wha—"

Haley was interrupted when Christian aggressively forced her back on the loveseat. Before she could try to run away, he crawled on top of her, forcing his weight on her.

"Wait! Christian! What are you doing?" she yelled, fighting with all her might, punching and pushing him back from her.

"You wanted this! You made me do this! This is all your fault!" he screamed, trying to dodge her hands and feet.

"No . . . please . . . no . . . don't do this!" she cried, feeling so little in this vulnerable situation.

"I'll show you how much I love you! You'll never think of leaving me again!"

Christian's hand moved toward her blouse, struggling to remove it. Frustrated, he slapped Haley, making her cry more hysterically. Her left cheek was throbbing; the impact of the slap left a slight cut on the corner of her mouth. She turned her head to the side, unable to bear that Christian was trying to rape her; her eyes were about to close in defeat when she saw the glass lamp on the side table.

If only I could reach it, Haley thought. She shifted her focus toward Christian; *I need to get him off of me!* Christian, not knowing about

Haley's ulterior motive, placed kisses on her body. *Just . . . a little bit more*, she extended her hand to grab the lamp while trying to get him off of her. *Finally!* Grasping the lamp in her hand, she drew it above her head and smashed it on his head.

Thud.

Christian dropped motionless on her shivering body, his hands limp on his sides. She shook him a little, and, when he didn't respond, she shoved him to the floor. Panicking, Haley collected her things, slipped on her blouse, and exited the house.

After that incident, Haley was depressed; she worried about what might happen to her. The smallest jolt made her jump and hyperventilate. Her appetite was decreasing, which worried Ross. He tried to ask what was wrong, and if he could help her in any way, but she would only weep at his question. Eventually, she told Ross about the affair and the attempted rape, and he could not believe it.

Christian was silent for the next couple of years; Haley hoped he'd forgotten about her. But, deep inside, she knew it was the calm before the storm. Her worries multiplied one day when she was walking back from the grocery store.

There was a hush in the wind; the street was eerily quiet, with only the moon's light illuminating the dark, cold night. Haley glanced at her watch; it said nine o'clock. *Why is it so quiet right now? It isn't so late, is it?* she thought. A cold shiver went across her spine. Her instincts were screaming at her: something was wrong. She had to get out of there. The stomping of boots in the dead of night startled her, and she halted. The sound was gone. Haley waited a few seconds and then took a few steps. No sound. Sighing, she walked toward her street. *Just a turn, and I'll be there.*

Stomp. Stomp.

Gasping, Haley turned around to look at the intruder. That was a mistake. A guy clad in black was staring back at her coldly. They stared, still, gauging each other, playing a game of cat and mouse.

Haley lost. She hastily ran toward her house, praying Ross would rescue her. She was a block away from her house when leather-gloved hands clamped on her waist and tried to drag her back.

"Ross!" she screamed, "Ross—"

"I told you!" the guy sneered, his lips beside her ear. "You can never leave me, Haley! You'll always be mine!"

Shocked, her eyes widened. She realized that the guy was none other than Christian.

"Chris . . . tian . . ." she murmured, terrified.

"Yes, babe! Who else would love you this much? I'm the only one who could be with you!" he roared, kissing her on the neck.

"Ross!" she hopelessly yelled again. "Ross!"

Christian was aghast when the front door opened. "Haley?" A shout came from the silhouette figure.

Alarmed, Christian pushed Haley aside and escaped before Ross could catch him.

"Haley! Are you okay?" Ross hugged her, stroking her back to calm her down.

"I . . . am . . . y . . . yes . . . s," she stuttered, pressing herself more into his embrace.

"Come on, let's get you inside and settled down." He took her inside the house.

From the trees, Christian glared at them, his hands clenched around a knife. Hot red blood trickled down his hand to the ground from where he'd cut himself. He was fuming, seeing the couple's display of affection.

If we cannot live together, we could die together. Till death do us part! Christian thought, vowing to himself, smirking darkly.

Chapter 5 – Nancy

Crash. The glass shattered on the floor, leaving behind pieces of shards everywhere. From an outsider's view, it would seem nothing but a mere glass breaking, but only the fuming couple knew the crack in the glass symbolized their ruined marriage. Brooke, their teenaged daughter, was hiding behind the opened door, peeking at her parents, scared and shaken, as her parents were fighting again for no real reason.

"I don't know what's wrong with you!" Adam yelled. "You were never so aggravated!"

"Me?" she screamed. "You're the problem! You've been treating me this way!"

"Your mother's death has taken a toll on you! You've completely lost it!"

"It did not!"

"It did. You're behaving like a little kid, throwing an unnecessary tantrum."

"You know what? I don't care what you think about me! Do whatever you want. I'm out!" Nancy picked up her bag and stormed out of the house.

"Yes! Go! We don't need you!" Adam's loud voice could be heard flowing in the wind.

The couple had been continuously fighting with each other since Ellie's death. The small quarrels were now turning into full-blown fights, leaving their mouths and hearts bitter. *It's been two years, and he's still arguing about this! Can't I even remember my mother?* Nancy thought. *Anyway, I should concentrate on meeting my girlfriends!* A smile spread on her face; Nancy was looking forward to meeting her old high school friends again. It wasn't a long ride; Nancy reached the place in fifteen minutes. It was a vintage-themed café with both outdoor and indoor seating areas. The exterior of the café was made up of brown rusted blocks with railings on both the left and right sides. A short handrail greeted Nancy when she walked toward the café entrance.

"Oh gosh! Seriously . . . ."

Chatter and laughter echoed around the café. The warm atmosphere was filled with the sweet smell of freshly baked goods. Nancy felt calm and refreshed at the café. *Finally, I can breathe peacefully!* She thought.

"Hey, Nancy!" a voice shouted. Nancy turned toward the left, where the voice seemed to be coming from. Three girls were seated near the window seat, and, among them, Nina was eagerly waving her hand to Nancy. "Over here."

Nancy went toward her friends. The quartet were friends from high school days; there was Nina, Amy, and Jade. Nina had blue eyes and curly blond hair; she was a teacher by profession. Amy was a veterinarian with black eyes and short brown hair, while Jade, the owner of the café and Nancy's best friend, had green eyes and crimson red hair.

Nancy had always been bisexual but had a stronger attraction to women. She knew her mother would not approve of her being in a relationship with a woman, so she never pursued one. However, she'd had a crush on Jade since they were in high school; she always admired her and felt giddy whenever she interacted with Jade, her insides turning mushy.

"Hey!" Nina said to Nancy enthusiastically.

"Hello!" Nancy replied.

"Look at you, girl; you look so exhausted," Amy said, worried.

"Ah! It's a long story, Amy. I'll tell you some other day." Nancy changed the topic. "Anyway, how about you people? How are you doing?"

"I had a long trip with my husband," Amy gushed. "We went on a vacation to Hawaii."

"Oh damn!" Nina shrieked. "That's my dream vacation! I wish I could go with my boyfriend; he's so busy nowadays." Her friends laughed at her childishness.

"What about you, Jade? Any adventure in your life?" Nancy asked Jade.

"I couldn't take a break. The café is getting more customers now; it gets so hectic around here. I'm worn out by the time I shut down," Jade whined.

"Don't worry, love. It'll get better soon." Amy comforted her while the other nodded.

"I guess so."

"Oh, have you heard . . . .?" The conversation continued. The girls were so excited to meet one another after so long that they didn't notice the time. It was late in the evening, and they had to part ways unwillingly. Nancy was the last one to leave, helping Jade clean up the tables.

"Alright, girl. Go on, speak your mind," Jade said, as soon as they were alone in the café. "I know something is bothering you."

Nancy smiled faintly, knowing no one could understand her better than Jade.

"Actually, the thing is . . . ." Nancy relayed all of it to Jade—her worries, her troubles, and her pain.

"Hmm . . ."

It was past midnight when Nancy reached her house. She didn't know her conversation with Jade would take this much time. She was completely out of it and needed peace in her life right now.

"So, you're finally home?" She heard Adam say, once she entered the living room.

"Huh?" Nancy was surprised to see him waiting for her. "Why are you up at this time?"

"I was worried about you; you've never been this late." He'd cooled off.

"Why are you exaggerating?" She rolled her eyes.

"I am not exaggerating! You're the one who's being insensitive about everything!"

"Look, I'm tired right now. Can we have this baseless conversation in the morning?"

"Baseless? Do you think it's baseless? I cannot even worry about my wife?"

"No! You can't! I don't want you to, alright?"

"What do you want then?"

"I know what to do now. I want a divorce."

"W . . . what . . . Nancy . . . what are you talking about?"

"I said I want a divorce!"

"Babe, look. I think we're misunderstanding each other. Just talk it out right now. Let's resolve it."

Nancy shook her head, tearing up. She marched up the staircase, leaving Adam pleading for her.

Adam was troubled by this. After all, he'd been with Nancy since their early twenties. Although Ellie forced them to get married when Nancy became pregnant with Brooke, Adam did truly love her.

*****

"I can't believe it! How can he blame me for everything? Why am I the only one responsible for this broken marriage?" Nancy muttered angrily to Jade, who was pacing back and forth in front of her.

It had been three weeks since she'd filed for the divorce and moved in with Jade. Her family and daughter kept calling her, asking her to return and give Adam a chance, but she dismissed them.

"Calm down, Cy," Jade said, calling her by her nickname.

"How can I? He ruined my life! If mother hadn't forced me to marry him, I would've never married that guy!" she cried out.

"I know. But it's over now, right? Stop stressing yourself so much!"

"I . . . c . . . cannot . . . believe I'm going to divorce him. I knew . . . we ha . . . ad . . . problems . . . but . . . I . . . nev . . . never . . . thought . . . it . . . wi . . . would . . . come . . . to . . . to this." Nancy began to bawl excessively.

"Shhh . . .." Jade embraced Nancy in her arms.

"I . . . thought . . . he . . . would . . . understand . . . me . . . but . . . I—" She couldn't speak anymore; her hiccups interrupted her.

Jade continuously patted her on the back; her arms tightened around her. It was heartbreaking for her to watch her best friend suffer like this. Consoling and sympathizing with Nancy was the only thing Jade could think of right now.

"Okay, calm down, girl." Jade leaned back from the embrace and lifted her face. "Look at me," she told Nancy. When Nancy didn't do as she was told, Jade called her again. "Look at me, Nancy," she firmly said.

"Darling, you're a brave woman! It isn't your fault that your relationship with Adam didn't work. It was bound to go this way. You need to let it go and move on." She comforted her.

Jade didn't know how close she'd gotten to Nancy while soothing her, but Nancy was aware of their distance. Jade was only one breath away from her. An adrenaline rush went through Nancy's body when she glanced back and forth from Jade's eyes to her lips. Nancy's eyes fixated on Jade's mouth when she parted her lips to speak. Jade continued speaking, clueless of Nancy's intention. Unconsciously, Jade licked her lips slowly to wet her dry and cracked mouth.

Nancy gulped, panting heavily. *I can't wait any longer; this is torture!* She leaned forward and kissed Jade. Jade's eyes widened in shock first, and, when she saw Nancy wasn't going to stop, she gave in and kissed her back. Their tongues clashed with each other, trying to dominate the other. Eventually, Nancy overpowered Jade. Jade whimpered at Nancy's dominance while Nancy's hand moved over Jade's body urgently.

Jade broke from the aggressive make-out session and tilted her head back, panting heavily. Out of breath, Nancy stared at Jade, her eyes dark with desire. She inclined toward Jade again, but Jade jumped up from the couch.

"Wait! Let's talk it out first, Cy."

"What's there to talk about? I want you, and you want me. That's it!"

"But Nancy—"

"No buts, Jade! Don't you think I've seen you giving me those glances? I know you're attracted to me. It's been this way since high school."

"I know, but . . . ." she trailed off, doubtful. Her gut feeling was telling her something wasn't right, and she shouldn't be in a relationship with Nancy.

"Come on, babe. We've known each other inside-out for a long time. What could possibly go wrong?"

"You're right. I guess I was just paranoid." Jade ignored her intuitions.

"That's my girl!" Nancy hugged Jade, caressing her hair. "I'm glad we're dating." She grinned at Jade and kissed her—little did they know that Jade's instinct was a sign of the darkness that would bring hell to their lives.

A year later, Nancy was seated across from Adam with their lawyers. Adam looked troubled, his tie undone and his face drained of any emotions while Nancy was delighted. And why wouldn't she be? After all, she was finally being freed from this forced marriage.

"Nancy, love. Please think about this again. We can make our marriage work." Adam requested her.

Nancy remained quiet. She was resolute in her decision.

"Please think about Brooke, Nancy . . . ."

Nancy sighed; she was done with the paperwork. *I'm free now! I can do whatever I want. There'll be no one to control or try to dominate me*, she thought. *Now I can focus on my Jade.*

Ever since her separation from Adam, Nancy had been living with Jade. To celebrate the divorce being final, the couple agreed to meet at a restaurant/bar they went to when they were younger. The bar was located near the suburbs, so it was easy to get there. It was a luxurious bar that served unlimited hors d'oeuvres to their customers. The bar's purplish-blue light greeted Nancy when she entered the building. *It's been so long! I wonder if anything has changed,* she thought. She gleefully scanned the area, searching for Jade. Nancy smiled after locating her sitting in a secluded booth and strolled toward her.

"Hey!" Jade locked her gaze with Nancy and greeted her, grinning widely.

"What the hell are you wearing?" Nancy sneered, her voice inaudible due to the loud music.

"What . . . what are you talking about? I can't hear you?" Jade questioned her.

"I said what the hell are you wearing?" Nancy shouted this time.

"Ah! Um . . ." Jade trailed off, looking down at her dress. It was a slim tight black dress that flowed to her knees. *Didn't she love this dress when I wore it two months ago? Why is she reacting like that?* Jade thought, puzzled.

"You look absurd in this dress! Could you be any sluttier?" Nancy was enraged.

"Sl . . . sl . . . slutty?" Jade's lips wobbled, tears emerging from the corners of her eyes.

"Oh for God's sake!" Nancy brushed her hands on her face, groaning. "Alright . . . alright, stop crying. I won't say anything now." She wiped her tears and kissed her on her forehead.

Seeing that Jade had calmed down, Nancy breathed a sigh of relief. "Come on, let's dance." Nancy took her to the dance floor, entangling her body with her. She pushed herself at Jade and made out with her. Jade felt a little uncomfortable with the public display of affection. However, she knew if she stopped Nancy, she might get upset, so she went along with it and tried to keep up with Nancy's kisses.

*****

Nancy glanced at Jade, serving an order to a customer. *Why is she smiling so pleasantly? Can't she see me sitting right in front of her?* She thought, scowling when Jade laughed at something the customer said.

Jade noticed Nancy's sharp gaze on her and smiled at her warmly. But she became worried when Nancy's scowl deepened. *What's wrong with her? Why is she making that expression? Is she bored? But she volunteered to be here; I didn't force her to.* Jade thought naively.

From the opening to the closing of the café, Jade felt uncomfortable with Nancy's behavior. Nancy would glare at anyone who came in close proximity to Jade and would continue to do so until that person exited the café.

That evening, while being nervous, Jade tried to unlock the gate of her house, her hands fumbling with keys. An irritated Nancy snatched the keys from her hands and unlocked the gate violently. She stormed inside the house immediately, leaving Jade at the front door. Jade sighed and followed her inside. This had been going on for the past few weeks; Nancy's startling change in behavior had Jade tiptoeing on broken glass.

Nancy was like a ticking bomb; no one knew when she'd blow up!

"I didn't know you would be this bold!" Nancy taunted her as soon as she stepped inside.

"What the heck are you talking about?" Jade said tiredly.

"Oh! So now you're behaving as if you don't know!" Nancy shouted.

"Nancy, stop!" Jade exclaimed. "I don't understand what's wrong with you! Why are you behaving like this?"

"Why am I behaving like this?" she yelled. She tightly grabbed Jade by her shoulders and shook her roughly. "This is all your fault!"

"Are you crazy?" Jade shoved Nancy. "Move. I don't want to talk to you right now!"

"No!"

"Ugh! I can't do this anymore. I regret meeting you again. I wish I didn't love you. I want to break—"

Smack.

The loud sound vibrated the dark, cold room. Jade lifted her quivering hand to her left cheek, a red handprint on it. Tears slowly started flowing from her eyes, anger washing with them, leaving behind nothing but numbness.

"Shhh . . ." Nancy wrapped her arms around Jade. "Look what you made me do! I told you to never talk about leaving me, didn't I?"

Jade sobbed, her eyes screaming and her heart bleeding. She knew there was no way out. Actually, Jade didn't want to be without Nancy; she was entangled in the spider's web now. She was in love with Nancy, and, truth be told, Nancy did treat her like a queen most of the time, but, with her, you could never be sure. One small thing would trigger Nancy, and when she got in one of her moods, you'd have hell to pay.

*****

Jade had been a little lost these past few days. It came out as a shock to her the first time Nancy slapped her; she couldn't imagine Nancy acting like this. *Why is she like this?* Jade thought, sighing, as she hung her clothes in the closet. She glanced at the clock and let out a sigh in relief; she still had an hour left before Nancy would get home. Nancy would always let Jade know where she was, but this time she didn't tell her where she was going or when she'd be back. When Jade woke up that morning, Nancy was already gone.

It eased her that she didn't have to force herself to face Nancy like she'd been doing for the past few days. There was tension between them after the incident; the couple had fewer interactions. Nancy too had noticed a change in Jade's behavior; she'd be on guard whenever she was around

94

her. She'd stutter and babble incoherent words, making Nancy annoyed. If Nancy tried to be affectionate with her, Jade became distant with her. And the further Jade pushed her away, the greater Nancy's frustration would become.

One day, Nancy asked her the reason behind her demeanor; she pretended as if there was nothing wrong between them and it was all in Jade's mind.

"Is there anything I can do to reduce this gap between us, babe?" Nancy inquired.

"I don't know, Nancy," Jade whispered. "The damage has been done; I don't know if anything could help us get back to normal."

"What damage? Are you mad at something?"

Jade remained quiet. Her silence spoke louder than her words ever could.

"Wait a minute! Are you still angry about that day? Huh?"

"Please, Nancy," she said. "I'm tired of the same question again and again. Let's end this conversation now. I don't want to talk about it anymore."

Since then, Nancy had been quiet; she didn't ask Jade anything. *Now that I think of it, her attitude was slightly weird,* Jade thought. *Is she planning something?* Her eyes widened, terrified. *Oh My God! What have I done? Have I awakened the devil again?*

Creak.

The groaning of the door startled Jade; panicking, she snuck a glimpse at the clock. It was half-past three in the evening;

"Jade!" Nancy shouted excitedly, her loud voice echoing to their bedroom. "Come down, babe!"

"Coming!" Jade yelled nervously.

Alerted, Jade advanced toward the stairs, her pace slower than usual. She hid her trembling hand behind her back and took a deep breath before moving toward the living room to face Nancy.

"There you are!" Nancy grinned, her hand hiding something behind her back. "I have a surprise for you!"

"W . . . what is it?" Jade stammered.

"This!" Nancy moved her hands and presented a bouquet of flowers to Jade. Her abrupt movement made Jade flinch, but, seeing the flowers, she relaxed. Nancy chose to ignore her actions. "Come on, love. Take it!" she said, pushing it to Jade, beaming.

"Thank you." Jade took the bouquet in her hands, gazing at them lovingly. The vibrant color of the purple hyacinth and flowery smell left her smiling. A teardrop slid from her left eye when she remembered the meaning of these flowers. "T . . . t . . . this . . . ." Jade's lips trembled, and she stared at Nancy.

"The purple hyacinth means forgiveness and sorrow, representing regret," Nancy whispered, lowering her head. "I'm sorry, Jade. Please forgive me, love." Nancy began crying, "I didn't—"

Jade engulfed Nancy in her arms tightly, interrupting her. The couple sobbed heavily, tears washing away with the bitterness in their hearts. The distance between them was reduced, and their souls became one once again.

"Are you still mad?" Nancy asked.

"No," Jade murmured.

"That's a relief then." Nancy leaned back and stared at Jade. "I have one more surprise for you!"

"What is it now?" Jade questioned, chuckling.

"Hmm . . . ." Nancy put her hand under the chin and pretended to think. "You'll find out, babe!" She winked at Jade. "Come on, let's go!"

"Wait. Wait." Jade stopped Nancy and pointed toward herself. She whined: "Just look at me; I need to change. How can I go out like this, Cy?"

"Ugh!" Nancy groaned. "Alright, go, but you only have ten minutes."

"Yes, mam!" Jade shouted, excited, and raced to the bedroom, leaving Nancy to snicker at her naiveté.

Nancy exhaled, happy that her love had forgiven her. She was worried Jade might never love her again and had been going crazy trying to find a way to show how much she regretted her actions. She always had a problem with her temper and would get angry even at small things. It was difficult for her to make friends in school; kids usually didn't want to be around her. It lowered her self-confidence; she became quiet and reserved.

*****

Nancy thought about a conversation she had with Haley a few hours earlier. Haley had been noticing the change in Nancy's behavior and confronted her about it. Nancy admired her older sister's courage and confidence; she wanted to be like Haley, but their mother would ultimately shun her.

"You know, Mom wouldn't approve of my divorce, nor would she approve of my relationship with Jade!" Nancy said to Haley.

"It's okay to be you; every person has his or her own life to live. It's not necessary for everyone to approve of you. You need to be you and love who you are. You're doing great, Nancy! I know the divorce was hard. Don't lose hope only because people don't appreciate you enough. Just do what you think is right, and people will love you for who you are," Haley advised her.

Her sister's counseling worked as a cure for Nancy's wounded heart, increasing the respect she had for her. She was the only one who understood Nancy. Nancy was a lonely child who craved love and attention from others, and Jade was the first friend who made her believe in herself.

She was and will always be special to me, my one and only! Nancy thought.

"Alright, I'm back!" Jade exclaimed, marching down the stairs. *Jade looks radiant as ever!* Nancy thought, staring at her from head to toe. She was wearing a purple summer dress with butterfly sleeves, and she paired it with black wedges.

"Let's go." Nancy took Jade's hand and intertwined it with hers.

"Where are we going?" Jade inquired as soon as they stepped out of the front door.

"I'm not gonna tell you, babe." Nancy peered at her. "I told you it's a surprise! Please don't ruin it."

"Fine! Fine!" She grumbled.

The trip to the surprise destination was spent reminiscing about when they were in school—the tears and laughs they shared, the sweet, fun moments that made their bond strong.

Is this the way to the forest? Jade thought, gazing outside the car window. The lush green tree and the damp moss smell greeted them as soon as Jade rolled down the window. *It's been ages since I was outside like this*, she smiled.

Peeking at Jade from the corner of her eyes, Nancy was glad to see that Jade was enjoying the landscape. The forest had always been the couple's getaway; they used to come here whenever they had troubles in their relationship and wanted to rant to each other for hours. Both of them loved how the breathtaking view and atmosphere of nature calmed them down.

"So, this was the surprise?" Jade turned toward Nancy, beaming. "Is this why we're here?"

"Yes and no," Nancy replied, trying to suppress her smile. "You'll find out soon, babe!"

Jade exhaled, frustrated. She kept glancing around the trees to search for the mysterious "surprise" Nancy had prepared for her. But when she couldn't, defeatedly, she went back to gaze at the trees. Nancy faintly chuckled at Jade's actions.

After half an hour, they were driving on a short road in the forest. Jade was surprised to see the newly constructed road. *It wasn't there the last time I visited*, she thought.

"This road has been recently constructed." Nancy clarified, knowing Jade was getting curious. "My brother Trinity built it for his new venture in the forest. It's a short road leading to an entertainment park."

"Oh!" Jade absorbed the new information, gaping at the beauty of the new construction. Loud chatter voices, the sweet aroma of food, and brightening colored lights were becoming visible to the couple now as they grew closer to their destination; Jade's curiosity increased.

"We're here," Nancy declared, turning off the engine. The trees opened up to a large clearing with a river flowing on its left side. On the right side, there were five food trucks busy serving the crowd their orders. Jade gazed in the middle, where people with their families and friends were sitting on many small square-shaped blankets, enjoying the ambiance and listening to a band playing music.

"I convinced my brother to name this place 'Blue Jade.' Did you know a blue jade represents inner peace and encouraging dreams? What do you think?" Nancy asked, staring at her.

"He named it after me?" "It's beautiful, Nancy!" Jade gushed. "I've never been to a place like this! Thank you for taking me out, babe." She engulfed Nancy in her arms and kissed her, appreciating the sweet gesture.

"I wasn't sure if you'd like it," Nancy murmured, leaning back from the kiss. "I wanted to show you I truly regret what I did that day; I promise I'll never do it again."

"I know." Jade stared into her eyes, showing Nancy she trusted her. "I love you."

"I love you too." Nancy reached out her hand to Jade and said, "Come on. Let's go."

The couple walked, hand in hand, trying to decide which food truck to visit first. Jade thought, *what an amazing day!*

*****

Months had passed since their visit to Blue Jade. Then one day, it happened . . . .

"I." Punch.

"Told." Kick.

"You." Slap.

"To." Punch.

"Listen to." Kick.

"Me." Slap.

Nancy moved away from the bruised and battered Jade, lying on the floor. Jade's hair was disheveled; her mouth had cuts, and her eyes were swollen from the punch. Her arms and legs had purplish-black marks from the previous beating she'd received.

"Come on! Get up!" Nancy barked. "You're such a bitch. You should be thankful I'm with you! Nobody would bother to even look at you. I'm the only one who loves you!"

Jade grimaced, lifting herself.

After the first incident, this had become a routine. Nancy would get triggered by little things and blow all of it at Jade. She was verbally abusive, physically abusive, and she humiliated her. At times, she even raped Jade. She didn't care if she was right or wrong or if Jade was hurt; she just wanted to show her dominance. She wanted Jade to obey her, no matter what and controlled her as she wanted. She was becoming obsessive and overprotective. Jade had thought about leaving her many times, but she loved Nancy, and, despite this treatment, she wanted to be with her. She felt like she could take this abuse since, most of the time, Nancy showed her love like no other person ever had.

I hate that she makes me do this to her! It's her fault!! Nancy thought to herself.

*****

A year had passed with no abuse from Nancy, and then one morning . . . .

Crash.

The glass breaking broke Nancy out of her thoughts. She sauntered toward the kitchen to investigate and was furious to see her favorite mug broken. Jade knew what was about to come and was shivering relentlessly.

"What's wrong with you!"

"I . . . I . . . I—"

"Will you speak or just keep on stuttering?"

"Uh . . . um . . . ."

"You won't." She affirmed. "Let me show you what happens when you mess with me!"

"No . . . no. Nancy, please! No!"

Ignoring Jade's pleas, Nancy, pushed her to the floor, tearing her blouse. She squeezed Jade's jaw to the point where it became painful and sore.

"Look what you make me do to you!" Nancy screamed. "Do you hear me? Look. What. You. Make. Me. Do. To. You!" she yelled, emphasizing every word specifically.

Jade's cries and whimpers could be heard across the whole house. Nancy stopped and sat next to Jade on the floor, saying, "I'm sorry, I love you, and this will never happen again. I need you! I love you!"

Jade had heard that apology before and knew it would not be the last time she heard it.

Nancy turned to Jade, seeing the tears and bruises on her face. She said, "Will you marry me?"

Chapter 6 – Trinity

Three years after the death of Ellie Peak, the FBI began an investigation of Trinity Peak's construction company for fraud. Trinity's company received a huge government contract shortly after Ellie's death, and he immediately began inflating building and material costs. Trinity had been playing cat and mouse with the FBI for years, and they couldn't find a way to get any evidence or witnesses to prove his crimes.

*****

The bar was swarmed with people dancing, eating, drinking, and smoking hookah. The red and black theme of the bar created a forbidden, intoxicating, and mysterious environment. Trinity observed his surroundings; he'd recently broken up with the previous flavor of the month and was on the lookout for a new one. Alas! None of the girls caught his eye.

His mind had lately been occupied by the FBI and the media's accusation of fraud. He was irritated and frustrated to see them accusing him without what he considered "any real evidence." Ellie helped him start the construction company years earlier, and only he and Ellie knew how the company began in the first place. Ellie and Trinity financed his

107

company through dark money and used it as a front to launder money for friends and clients.

Do they know how hard it was for me and what I had to endure when I was struggling to start this company?

Days before, he'd gone through an interrogation. The FBI agents were not convinced by whatever came out of his mouth, but they couldn't do much because of a lack of evidence. They needed to prove his fraud, and Trinity only mocked and insulted them, fueling the already lit flame between them.

"Oh! Are you here to arrest me, agent? No? Oh, right! How would you, agent? You don't have the evidence to arrest me."

Trinity sighed, chuckling and recalling the interrogation and the agent's expressions.

He gulped the last bit of whiskey and made his way to the bar. Once there, he signaled the bartender for a refill. He was waiting for his drink when a girl clad in a royal blue strapless dress came to sit beside him.

"One more, please," she asked the bartender. The girl had a beautiful complexion, emerald eyes, and straight blonde hair. She was tall, lean, and in her mid-30s. *Damn it, boy!!* Trinity thought, smirking.

"How long are you gonna stare at me?" The girl, who'd been feeling his penetrating gaze on her suddenly turned toward him.

"Until you say yes." He joked, making her roll her eyes.

"Hi! I'm Trinity." He stretched his hand out.

"Hello! I'm Kristen." She shook his hand.

"So . . . who are you with? I mean, are you here alone or with your friends?"

"I came here with my friends." She scanned the dance floor. "But I have no idea where they are now."

"Oh! That's too bad. I feel sorry for you." Both of them knew that he didn't feel so; he was rather elated about it. "Don't worry about it; I'll keep you company tonight." Kristen could see the promise in his eyes.

"Sure, I'd love to be in your company."

Trinity laughed.

For the next two hours, they stuck together, conversing, flirting, and teasing each other. Kristen told Trinity she was in the city for a week; she was visiting a friend and staying in a hotel.

"So, how do you like the city?" Trinity asked her.

"Hmm . . . ." She paused, deliberating. "It seems okay to me, I guess."

"Just okay?" He lifted his eyebrow in question.

"I've only been here for what, two days? How would I know in such a short time?" She shrugged.

"Ah . . . you're right. How about you explore the city with me?"

"Let's see . . . ."

The more Kristen and Trinity opened up about each other, the more their desire burned. There was an invisible sexual tension between them. Trinity wanted to know as much about her as he could. He wanted her, and he was going to get her by any means necessary. The two were playing a dangerous game, giving each other meaningful glances, touching each other's hands not-so-accidentally—plus the occasional deep eye stare. They were waiting for the other to take the initiative, being stubborn in their own ways.

"Why don't we go somewhere else?" Trinity surrendered. "The bar is getting overcrowded."

"Where?" she asked.

"How about my place? We can drink and just chill."

"Hmm . . . sure."

This was his go, the moment he was waiting for. He didn't wait for a single second; clasping his hand in hers, he raced to the car. The driver was alerted by Trinity's presence, and he immediately unlocked the car.

"Where to, sir?" the driver asked.

"Take us back home and pull up the partition," Trinity ordered.

"Yes, sir."

Now that he was sure the driver couldn't listen or watch them, he pulled Kristen close. Her dress got hiked up due to her new position, making him look down at her. *Fuck! I want you!*

"Unh. Unh. Unh." She teased him, waving her fingers back and forth. "Have a little patience, darling. We wouldn't want the driver to be distracted now, do we?"

Trinity kissed her passionately; he wanted to consume her in that kiss, but Kristen wasn't one to back down, and she fought with him as feverously as she could. The two were on fire, wanting the other to burn with them.

Panting, they broke from the kiss; Trinity placed kisses down her neck and followed the path with his tongue. He probed around her neck, placing deep kisses everywhere to find her love spot. Kristen gasped. *Found it!* Trinity thought, grinning deviously.

Licking.

Sucking.

Kissing.

Trinity kept repeating the process until a love bite started to form. He loved her moans and groans, her sharp intake of breath whenever he sucked hard, and her slow sweet whimpers. She was melting in his arms, and he was ready to make love to her.

They were both so engrossed in each other that they didn't hear the car engine stopping and signaling that they'd reached their destination.

"Sir?" the driver called, unsure.

"Huh?" Trinity said, dazed. He glanced outside the window and realized they were outside his penthouse apartment. Kristen lifted herself from his lap and stepped out of the car.

"Okay, you can go now. I'll call you tomorrow," Trinity told the driver, who nodded and started the engine again. Trinity guided Kristen to the private elevator, located at a different place than the common one, leaving her perplexed.

"Why are we using this elevator and not the usual one everyone is using?"

"You'll see." He pecked her, smirking.

As soon as the elevator opened, a single door with an initial 'T' on the other side became visible to them. He unlocked the door and motioned Kristen to enter. "After you."

Kristen laughed at his fake chivalry and stepped inside the apartment. She was astonished to see the apartment was decorated in a luxurious and extraordinary way. Trinity was proud to see her appreciating his place, but he didn't let her admire much before he lifted her up and sprinted to the master bedroom.

*****

Ring. Ring. Ring.

"Hello, Seth speaking," the male voice answered.

"Seth, it's me." A voice could be heard from the other side.

"Em? Where are you? Where did you go, and why didn't you let anyone know you were leaving? Do you know how worried we all were? Tell me where you are; I'm coming to get you now."

"Seth. Seth. Calm down! Relax, okay?" There was a pause. "I'm at his place, Seth."

A pregnant silence.

"Are you . . . are you out of your mind, Emily? Do you know how dangerous it is? God knows what he'll do if he discovers your identity. I don't know what the SAIC was thinking when he assigned you this case."

"I know you're worried about me, but remember your sister is braver and stronger than you think. I won't let anyone bring me down."

"I know, Em, but—"

"I know. Seth, I'm sending you some information I got my hands on. Can you please look into it for me?"

"Alright. Just take care of yourself, Sister."

"You too, Brother."

The phone hung up.

Seth was worried for his sister now. She didn't know what she'd gotten herself into, but Seth wanted to keep thinking the best for her.

*****

Trinity woke up the following day early in the morning, delighted from the ravishing lovemaking last night. However, his smile flipped to a scowl when he found the other side of the bed empty. *Where is she? Did she leave?*

He got up from the bed and walked out of the room in search of Kristen, picking up his white robe on the way. He searched in the bathroom; the area around the bathtub was clean and wet, as if someone had taken a bath just now. He was halfway through the hallway when he heard humming noises. Listening carefully to the voice and following the sound, he found Kristen cooking in the kitchen.

"Aren't you a little too happy in the morning?" He joked, leaning against the door.

"Haven't you heard the quote 'early to bed early to rise?'" She teased, turning toward him.

"I have . . . but I prefer late nights and late mornings." There was a mischievous twinkle in his eyes that showed Kristen what he really meant.

"I guess you're right, Mr. Trinity."

They both chuckled.

After the breakfast, Trinity suggested Kristen spend her last week in the city with him rather than going back to her hotel. This way, she could live in a comfortable and nice environment without worrying about any expenses. Oh and sex was the cherry on the top!

Initially, Kristen declined his offer, probably because she felt embarrassed or something. However, Trinity's stubbornness lifted her resolve, and she finally agreed to stay there. They both knew it was a fling, just casual sex with no strings attached.

"My phone is on the counter. Do me a favor and call my driver to let him know I'm on my way down."

"Your phone is locked," Kristen told him.

"Oh, the code is 0419," Trinity replied.

"Those are really random numbers," she said.

"I know, it's the date I closed on my first big project, Q Towers," he explained.

"I'll be back soon; feel free to explore." He nibbled her lips and moved back. "But the study room is off-limits."

"Don't worry; I won't step foot in there."

*****

"Seth, did you look into the files I sent you?" she asked on the call.

"I did, but this isn't enough to arrest him."

"Fuck!"

"Have you looked everywhere?"

"I'm in his study now. The room is so clean and organized I can't find anything out of order."

"Have you checked the drawers?"

"I've double-checked them!"

"Hang in there; I know you can find them."

"I'll call you back if I find anything."

"Okay."

*****

This one day during that week, Trinity cleared all his schedule to spend the day with Kristen. He had everything sorted out, and Kristen was unaware of the surprise he had planned for her. *I hope she likes it; after all, she's the only woman I would spend this much time with*, he thought.

"Kristen?" he shouted, pacing past the hallway.

"What?" Kristen appeared from the living room. "Why are you shouting?"

"I didn't see you," he muttered sheepishly. "I thought you left without saying goodbye."

"Don't worry, darling. I won't leave you without a farewell fuck." She flirted, winking at him.

"Mhm . . . ." Trinity put his arms around her waist and pulled her close, leaving no space between them.

"I don't know; I haven't heard of that practice before." He pretended to think and said, "Why don't we practice it before you leave town?"

"Umm . . . let's see," she remarked, teasing him. "I don't think— ah . . . ." Rolling his eyes, Trinity put her over his shoulder and sauntered toward the bedroom.

"Hey!" she shouted, kicking and punching him. "Put me down right this instant, Trinity." Trinity ignored her. "I said—"

Smack. Kristen's hip burned from the smack Trinity gave her. It wasn't a violent smack; Trinity had made sure not to hurt her physically. He wasn't a violent person and had never lifted his hand to any woman. Trinity knew the limits—to maintain personal space, which was the only thing he learned from his father.

"Shut up," Trinity said, exhausted from being kicked continuously. "We're almost there, love. Can you please stop trying hard to resist it?"

Kristen let her hair shield her face, embarrassed. Her face was on fire; the red blush was now visible. *The hell?* She thought. *This misogynistic man! Oh, you'll get it now! You messed with the wrong one, babe.*

Trinity dropped her on the bed and moved back to remove his shirt. Kristen saw this as an opportunity and crawled back, away from his reach. His smoldering eyes stayed on her while he lazily unbuttoned his shirt.

"Come here," Trinity said, motioning her with his eyes.

"No!" Kristen frowned, shaking her head. "We're not having sex."

"Kristen, please . . . ."

"No! Not before you say sorry to me."

"What?"

"Say sorry!"

"I've never said sorry to anyone, and I don't plan on saying it now."

"Alright, then!" Holding his stare, Kristen unfastened the string that was holding the front of her dress.

Trinity's eyes darkened when he witnessed she wasn't wearing her bra.

"I guess you don't want this." Teasing, Kristen went on tying it again. "It's okay. I should just—"

"Sorry," he whispered.

"What!" Kristen was shocked. Trinity, an arrogant and proud man who'd never bowed down to anyone had asked for forgiveness, even though it was only the lust talking right now. "What did you say? I didn't hear you."

"I said sorry, okay!" Trinity yelled, annoyed. "Just get it over with."

Yup, he's sexually frustrated, she thought, snickering. *Guess I'm going to be sore tomorrow too.*

"What are you laughing at?" he asked.

"Nothing," she said, beaming. Kristen crawled toward him seductively, the dress almost sliding down her body, making it bare to him. Trinity gulped slowly; she looked like a devil who'd burn him with her flames. He was still in his place, gauging her actions and trying to control his inner beast from taking her.

Reaching in front of him, Kristen positioned herself, now kneeling on the bed. Their eyes leveled. She glanced at his broad shoulder and chest; the sweat was glistening from his muscles, and she caressed them. As if she was memorizing it, Kristen's fingers stroked his chest slowly.

Trinity sharply took in a breath when her hand touched his chest. "Fuck!" he groaned; his patience was shattered now. In a flash, he leaned in and placed his mouth on hers, kissing her hard. The kiss showed the desperation and hunger they had for each other.

"Open your mouth!" He instructed her. Kristen kept her mouth shut, refusing to obey him. "Kristen. Open your mouth!" he growled darkly. *I need to handle this in another way,* he thought. *She won't respond if I get too aggressive.*

Trinity changed his tactics and approached her in a different way. He traced her body with his hands, groping and touching her everywhere. Inching closer to her chest, Trinity then "accidentally" slid his hand on her breast.

Kristen gasped; Trinity seized that moment. He shoved his tongue inside her mouth and resumed kissing her firmly.

"Come on, lay down," he mumbled against her mouth and gently removed her dress. Peering down at her body, Trinity gently pushed her back and crawled on top of her.

Trinity moved the hair covering her face, sliding his fingers in between her hair and face to feel the smooth, silky texture. He didn't know why, but he wanted to feel her soul more than the body. He wanted to make love to her and not just have the mindless sex they were accustomed to. Kristen could feel something had changed in him, but the question was what . . . and was he the only one who'd changed?

The next day Trinity woke up before Kristen; his eyes went straight toward her, gazing. It was an eventful night; the couple didn't have sex, but they spent the whole night cuddling and talking to each other.

It was the first time Trinity had ever experienced this moment; it wasn't just a physical attraction. That moment was more intimate than having sex. Trinity never took the time to care about the other person. He only cared about fulfilling his needs. So why now? What was going on with him? He himself didn't know!

"Kris?" Trinity poked her. "Kris, wake up!"

"Mhm . . . ." Kristen grumbled, swatting his hands. "Just two more minutes, please."

"Nope!" He traced out his name on her skin. "Wake up, babe. It's . . ." a quick glimpse at the clock on the nightstand, "eleven in the morning."

"No! I don't want to!" she groaned, turning to the other side. "Go away, Avery!" Avery was her ex-boyfriend.

Avery? Trinity thought, his eyes narrowing and the smile on his lips tightening. *Who the hell is he? And why is she calling his name? Is she fucking dreaming about him?* Trinity closed his hand in a tight fist.

"Who the hell is Avery?" Trinity asked, trying his hardest to calm down.

Kristen's eyes enlarged; she was wide awake now. She sensed danger from his tone, as she hadn't seen him so angry before. She was scared of the sudden hostility.

"He . . . he's my nephew," she told Trinity, turning toward him to observe his reaction.

"Nephew?" he inquired. "Didn't you tell me you were an only child?"

"Yes, that's true. I'm the only child." She confessed. "Avery is my best friend Casey's seven-year-old son. We often sleep over at each other's house, so he'd always wake me up like that."

"Oh, alright!" Trinity leaned forward and pecked her forehead. Wrapping his arms around her waist, he pulled her closer.

"Why? Do you doubt me?" Kristen pretended to be upset. "Don't you trust me?"

"No. No. It wasn't that," Trinity said, "I was just . . . ."

"Jealous?" She teased him.

"You wish!" He laughed. "Oh!" Yawning, he continued, "I forgot to tell you, I have a surprise for you!"

"Surprise?" Kristen said nervously. "What kind of surprise?"

"Won't the surprise be ruined if I tell you?" Trinity asked. "Just trust me, babe!"

"Alright." Kristen pulled the sheets off her and stood up from the bed, giving Trinity the opportunity to gaze at her body. "Just let me get dressed."

"Well . . . I won't mind if you go out like this." He joked, ogling her body and biting his lips.

"Oh really?" She taunted, looking at him from her peripheral vision. "I guess it'll be a treat to other men as well. Don't you think?"

Immediately, Trinity scowled and glared at her. Kristen laughed at his expressions, mimicking his scowl. His face relaxed when he realized she was just teasing him.

"Oh, you're going to get it now!" Trinity ran to catch her, which made Kristen run to the living room.

*****

Trinity's and Kristen's affair continued for the remaining time she stayed at his penthouse. They were glued to each other for a week; their hands couldn't get enough of each other. Trinity was glad to find a woman who didn't expect anything from him. That was the type of affair he looked for, and he finally got it. There wasn't anything they hadn't tried. From skinny dipping in the lake to slow sex in the shower, from having sex on the kitchen countertop to having a quickie in the closet, Kristen tried different ways to seduce him, and Trinity had fallen for each of them. He didn't question her flirting and over-the-top behavior.

Trinity was getting the best sex in his life; why would he care about other things? He wasn't worried anymore about the FBI's investigation of his company. It was as if Kristen distracted him, keeping him engaged in her so he wouldn't know what was going on behind him. Nobody could understand what was going on in Trinity's mind and what his next move would be. Whether it was his carefree attitude or over-confidence that would be his downfall, only time could tell.

The FBI had been at his back, following him and tracing his calls to find any evidence that could have him arrested—but to no avail.

It was like the more they tried to find evidence, the harder it became to get it. If Ellie taught Trinity one thing, it was how to cover his tracks.

Trinity started working on his new projects without any worry. He knew the FBI was going through everything he was doing and made sure not to do anything that made them suspicious of him. The best thing for him was a night of passion after a full day of exhaustion. He eagerly looked forward to the night in anticipation of what was to come. It wasn't love for him; it couldn't be. It was just a sweet, forbidden affair for him because Trinity never loved just one woman.

*****

"Wait, the portrait!"

"What? Emily! What portrait?"

Emily rushed over to the portrait.

"Oh my gosh! I can't believe it!"

"What's wrong? What are you so excited about? You're scaring me, Em!"

"There's a portrait of his mother on the wall, and I found the safe behind it, Seth!"

"What!"

"It's locked! How can I open it?"

"Okay. Okay, relax. Clue . . . look for a clue."

For an hour, the girl searched for a clue, rummaging through every file.

April 16 – Enterprise

June 23 – Maybell Departments

April 19 – Q Towers

She halted on the last file and went through its contents thoroughly, checking each and everything and memorizing the agreement in her mind.

Here goes nothing! She thought, determined.

"Seth, I think I know the code."

"Really? Then what are you waiting for? Just hurry up and get yourself out of there."

Nervously, Emily entered the number 0419 on the touch lockpad; it was the same code she used to unlock his phone. She waited for a few seconds, her heart beating fast with anticipation—then suddenly it opened.

Jackpot!

She took a flash drive out of the safe, made a copy, then put it back, placing it in the black bag and closing the safe. She then put the portrait back in place so as to not alert Trinity. She cleaned and organized the room and left it the way it was, exiting the penthouse.

"I'm coming back, Seth."

She hung up.

You just wait, Mr. Trinity Peak! Soon you'll be going down . . . .

*****

When Trinity arrived home that night, he didn't notice a single thing out of place. Kristen had told him in the morning that she'd be leaving that day. Trinity wished he could have made love one last time. He was a little disappointed his affair had to end; nevertheless, everyone knew his heart didn't stop for anyone. He would find another Kristen soon, but he couldn't stop thinking about her. No woman had ever made him feel this way.

Would he find someone else besides her? Was it just lust, or was it something else, something real?

Love? Trinity frowned, mumbling. *No way! Trinity Peak doesn't love; it was just a thing! Yes, she was nice and caring. The moments I spent with her were amazing, but I'd never fall in love! Huh! Foolish mind!*

Trinity kept on mumbling the same thing again and again. Was it the truth, or was he only trying to convince himself? Little did he know Emily/Kristen would be back in his life, but not the way he wanted her . . . .

Chapter 7 – Dean

At 10:00 p.m., Dean arrived at his house, exhausted from the rush hour at the hospital. Day by day, his life was changing, going from bad to worse. His mother's death had taken a toll on his emotional and mental condition. He wasn't the same as he used to be when Ellie was alive three years ago. He'd changed entirely; his behavior, lifestyle, and personality had dissolved into emptiness.

Dean didn't remember the last time he'd smiled or showered love upon his children. Dean knew he'd been neglecting his family; he'd continuously tried to overcome his sorrow but came back empty-handed, especially after taking the Benzo Albert gave him. Even though Dean knew of the side effects he kept taking dose after dose. He had now become addicted to Benzos; without them, he'd hyperventilate and shiver excessively.

"Dean, darling, is that you?" Kat's voice greeted him from the kitchen.

"Yeah, Kathrine," he replied.

He knew she didn't like being called Kathrine and only would answer to Kat.

"Are you alright? You've never been this late."

"The patients kept rushing in, and the hospital was in urgent need of doctors so I stayed back."

"Oh, okay. You should go and freshen up. I'll serve you dinner."

"Alright. Where are the kids?"

"The kids fell asleep while waiting for you."

Dean nodded.

He felt guilt and remorse for the way he treated his loving family, but nothing was in his control now; in fact, the drugs controlled him.

Kat watched her husband walking to the bedroom. She felt sad about his situation and somehow blamed herself. She thought if she could do something to stop him or understand his problems, he wouldn't have to suffer alone. Kat remembered the first time Dean had taken a Benzo and how he didn't know how to control himself. He'd be so heavy on those drugs he'd mindlessly shout at his kids.

When Kat had tried to stop him, Dean, who'd never raised his voice at her, lifted his hand to her. The red mark on her face pulled him out of the drowsy situation. The memory of that night still brought tears to their eyes whenever any of them talked, as they realized that the previous Dean seemed to be gone . . . and he was never going to come back again!

Kat got scared watching Dean's condition get worse by the day. She knew some irrevocable event was about to unfold in the near future.

The dinner had already warmed up when Dean came down; he'd changed to his comfortable PJs and uninterestingly eyed the dishes. Kat had prepared his favorite dishes.

"Come on, sit down," Kat said. She pushed him toward the chair. She watched Dean eat silently; this was how Kat loved him—the peaceful and calm Dean, the guy who'd picked her up from the floor and gave her immense love. But, alas, that Dean was lost somewhere.

"How was your day today?"

"Good."

"Did you have to attend too many patients today?"

"Just a little more than usual."

"Hmm . . . I was thinking, Dean . . . ."

"Yes?"

"Why don't we go away for a weekend?"

"We?"

"You, me, and the kids. It's been years since we last went out of the city or country. I think it would be good for all of us; think of it as a fresh start."

"A fresh start . . . ."

Dean repeated her words again and again. Kat was happy to see him agreeing to her plan. At last, things were finally looking up.

*****

"Syringe."

"Endoscope."

"Surgical scissors."

Dean was in the operating room; he was performing liver surgery with his fellow doctors and nurses. The surgery wasn't a new thing for him; he'd been performing surgeries for years now. He knew the procedures and equipment needed in surgery; why was his hand trembling so hard then? The only answer to that was " the drugs."

An hour earlier, Dean took two Benzos because he thought there wouldn't be any patients left, but he was wrong. Mr. Jake, a highly respected businessman and political figure was rushed in before Dean could leave for home. As most of the doctors had gone home and Dean was the only surgeon remaining, the case was transferred to him without much ado.

Dean wanted to decline, but he knew he couldn't, as Mr. Jake was an influential person; if the hospital staff and doctors neglected him, it would be chaotic.

"Doctor!" Dean, who was in a daze because of the drugs, snapped out of it when a nurse called him.

"Yes?"

"Doctor, something is wrong with the patient!"

"What?" Dean looked at the monitor. "Bring the defibrillator, hurry!"

"Here it is." The nurse outstretched the machine to him.

"Clear!" Dean placed the paddles on Mr. Jake's chest and repeated it two more times.

"Clear!"

"Clear!"

For half an hour, shouts and instruction were lodged from everywhere; the doctors and nurses were in a frenzy, but Dean didn't know what was going on. It was as if he was just physically there, and his mind was absent.

Beep.

An invisible current passed through everyone in the operating room when the zig-zag line on the monitor turned straight and plain, signaling the demise of a very important patient. It was a living nightmare for them; none of them knew how to explain what happened.

*****

The next day . . .

"Are you out of your mind? Do you know what you've done? Is this why we trusted you on this case?" Dr. Lucas, the chief surgeon, shouted at Dean.

"Do you have any idea what will happen now? How could you do this?" Caleb, the hospital's director, was also enraged.

"I . . . I'm sorry. I didn't know the drugs would turn everything upside down. If I knew something like this would happen, I wouldn't—"

"What did you say?" Caleb asked him. "Drugs? Were you on drugs?"

Dean went pale. It was then that he realized he'd dug his own grave.

"I . . . I . . . I mean . . . ."

"I can't understand this!" William, the hospital's chairman, took his head in his hands. "Can someone explain to me how it turned out like this?"

"I'm really disappointed in you, Dean!" Lucas expressed his displeasure. "I never would've thought a person I'm mentoring would turn into a drug addict!"

Embarrassed and guilty of his crime, Dean lowered his head and quietly listened to his superiors and mentors. He knew what they were saying was right; he'd made a grave mistake—one that could not be recovered from, no matter what.

"I don't think a person who abuses his profession should be given a right to work where he could become a danger to the people!" declared Dr. Troy, a medical board official, mutely listening to their conversation.

"I agree with you, doctor," Caleb said.

"Wa-a-i-it. What's going on?" Dean cried out.

"Dr. Peak, you are relieved of duty, and there will be an investigation!" Dr. Troy announced firmly.

"But, sir, please allow me a chance to explain—"

"Chance to explain? This is a homicide investigation now!"

"Pack your shit and leave the hospital premises now, please. You have one hour," Caleb said.

Dean knew he was in major trouble now . . . .

*****

Two years after the hospital incident, Dean was still under investigation. He'd been in a terrible mood, shouting and screaming, throwing things. His mind had shut down because of the incident. He even tried committing suicide several times, but Kat stopped him every time.

Why wouldn't she let me rest peacefully? Why does she want me to rot in this world? Why?

"Dean, listen to me!" Kat called out to him. "Everything will be alright, love."

He was aware that Kat only wanted the best for him, but her continuous nagging had him going crazy. The drug's effects made him feel as if she was trying to control and manipulate him, and that was why he committed horrendous acts that could not be undone. Something similar happened on that day too . . . .

"Dean? Babe, talk to me. I know what you're feeling—"

"You know how I'm feeling, huh?" He suddenly turned toward her and barked. He leaned on her, forcing her to move back on the couch.

"D-D-Dean . . . ."

"Do you?" he bellowed; his eyes were bloodshot from the Benzo he'd taken. He kept on pushing her down until there wasn't any space between them. Kat was sandwiched in between the couch and Dean; she was trying hard to breathe normally.

"Please, Dean!" She cried. "You're suffocating me."

"I'm suffocating you? Am I? So you also think you can accuse me?"

"Dean!" Kat shouted. "Snap out of it! Please."

Dean's drugged mind was enjoying her squirm below him; he loved the expressions she was making. He watched her for a minute or so; at that moment, he did something he'd never done before—something he never could've imagined himself doing. His hand traveled all over her body, pinching, squeezing, and groping. Kat was horrified; she knew where all this was going. She was aware that Dean was under the influence of drugs and alcohol, or else her Dean wouldn't even think of hurting her.

Kat relentlessly fought him, kicking and punching him to push him back; she wanted to run away from her ill fate. Dean was getting irritated by her reluctance. He captured both of her hands in one, and with the other, he continued to explore her body, ignoring her tears.

The hot tears flowed one after the other; not only had Kat lost Dean, but, for the first time in her life, she'd been raped!

Kat still loved Dean, and despite the rape and abuse she would not leave him.

*****

A year later . . .

"Dad!"

"Dad!"

"Dad!"

The shout resonated throughout the house. Dean's children kept shouting to get his attention; they were excited about finally getting to spend a day with their father.

Dean was tired of the screams, and the loud voice kept vibrating in his head. He felt as if someone was smashing his head with a hammer. Laying his head in his hands, he crouched down in a corner, trying to block every sound. *Where did Kat go? Did she have to go now? Was it really necessary? Why didn't she take the kids with her?*

"Dad, look: Ray is making fun of me," Ten-year-old Peter complained.

"I did not!" Eight-year-old Ray shouted. "It was all Blake's idea."

"Hey!" Blake, their fifteen-year-old brother, yelled, annoyed. "Don't involve me in your stupid arguments."

The kids continued shouting; their every word turned into a verbal fight. Dean, who was already heavily dosed and drunk, was irritated and fed up with the kids now.

Enough is enough! They need to stop! I have to stop them!

Dean's eyes fixated on the knife placed in the half-opened drawer. As if in a trance, his hand slowly moved toward it. His mind and conscience were screaming to stop; he was fighting an internal battle with himself, but he grasped the knife in his hand. He'd lost the battle and was not in his senses anymore. The drugs and alcohol had overpowered him completely.

I'm doing this for them, for their happiness. They'll be happy afterward . . . .

Dean turned toward them, smiling faintly. For the first time, Dean was thinking about killing his children. Thankfully, this time, he was able to stop himself.

Chapter 8 – Jonathan

"Suzanne!" Jonathan shouted, "Suzanne, hurry up. We're going to be late for the party!"

"I'm coming. I'm coming!" Suzanne shouted back. "Would you stop shouting? The kids will wake up again."

Suzanne didn't want Angie and Alex, their twin daughters, to come to her room because she knew they'd make her late.

"Oh, I didn't know . . . ." His eyes fixated on Suzanne's dress.

"What the hell are you wearing?" he furiously asked; there was a hint of jealousy in his voice.

"What?" She glanced at her gown. "What the hell is wrong with it?" The asymmetric white gown was a simple lace dress that highlighted her curves at the right places.

"I don't want you to wear that. Change into something decent."

"Decent? It looks pretty decent to me."

"I said . . . ." Jonathan clenched her jaw in his hand and squeezed her mouth. He leaned his face closer to her and repeated in an intimidating manner again. "Change. That. Fucking. Dress."

143

Jonathan shoved her face away from him; he felt a little remorse when he saw tears trickling down her cheeks "You've changed, Jonathan."

Jonathan didn't understand what she meant; to him, he was the same as he was before Ellie's death. *Nothing has changed in me; it's just people who didn't know me well enough!* He thought bitterly.

He didn't want to make his wife cry, nor did he want to ruin their night. The only thing Jonathan knew was that he couldn't let other people indecently eye his wife. Everyone knew how beautiful Suzanne was—it wasn't a secret. People always looked forward to seeing her at events—men and women both.

Jonathan hated it every time. He didn't want to share what was his; he was slowly turning into a controlling maniac like his mother. He wanted things, people, society, and also the world to be under his control.

"Is this dress okay, Jonathan?" Suzanne asked, exhausted, walking down the stairs.

"Hmm . . . ." He deliberately paused and observed her gown. The black dress had full sleeves, and it flowed to her knees. "Alright. This will do."

Finally! Suzanne thought, sighing in relief.

Jonathan's sharp eyes didn't miss her small movement, but he let it go this time. They were already late for the party, and he didn't want to waste any more time.

Ever since Ellie's death two years ago, Jonathan had been attending political parties and meetings. He was determined to win his mother's senate seat by hook or by crook. He knew what these parties meant for political figures and donors; they attended them not just to mingle with other people but also to look out and gauge people's strengths and weaknesses. And if a person was valuable, they'd create an alliance with them. Jonathan had learned from Ellie that, the more alliances you make, the more powerful you become!

The party was in full swing when the couple arrived at the venue; it was a lit outdoor event organized by a highly respected political donor, Mr. Hale. Jonathan wanted to form an immediate alliance with him; he was sure that having Mr. Hale on his side would help him win the senate seat. He knew Mr. Hale was a king in the making, and that he hated the governor.

"Remember what I told you in the car," he muttered to Suzanne. "Behave. Don't go overboard, got it?"

145

Suzanne nodded.

Jonathan watched Suzanne getting herself adjusted to the woman's circle; when he was satisfied she wouldn't misbehave, he went to find his latest target.

"Mr. Hale!" Jonathan greeted the host as politely as he could.

"Oh! Mr. Peak!" Mr. Hale was pleased to see Jonathan; he stretched out his hand toward him. "How are you, young man?"

"I'm good, sir." He firmly shook his hand. "How are you now? I heard from my assistant that you haven't been feeling well the past few days."

"What can I say? I'm getting old now." He chuckled. Jonathan chuckled with him, even though he didn't get what was funny.

More and more people gathered around the two, listening and giving their two cents. Jonathan was getting acknowledged and appreciated by many of Hale's peers and colleagues; it was more than what Jonathan had asked for.

Every once in a while, Jonathan would glance at his wife. He was keeping a watchful eye on her, afraid she might say the wrong thing or make a fool out of him.

146

Thank God, everything is going how I planned it, he thought, sighing.

Near the end of the party, Jonathan accomplished what he wanted. He was successful in arranging a meeting with Mr. Hale for the upcoming Monday. Now the senate seat wasn't that far from him.

Count your days, governor. I'm coming for you! He thought, grinning darkly.

*****

"You know, this wouldn't have happened if you weren't supportive." Jonathan clasped the diamond necklace on Suzanne's neck. He gazed at her in the mirror. "Do you like my gift?"

"I do." She outlined the diamond cutwork with her fingers. "It's very beautiful."

"Anything for my darling wife." He kissed her on the side of her forehead. Jonathan kept staring at her in the mirror, his eyes dark and smoldering.

Suzanne was unable to understand her husband's love for her and their family. One minute, he wanted to do everything and anything for them, and, the other, he wanted to control and manage them. She was disturbed by this sudden change in him; he was turning into her mother-in-law.

"What are you thinking about, darling?" Pushing her hair aside once more, Jonathan caressed the back of her neck with his nose, moving it back and forth. His arms wrapped tightly around her waist, holding her captive in that intimate position.

"Mhm . . . ." Suzanne involuntarily let out a moan.

Jonathan chuckled at her. He liked that his wife was oh-so-sensitive and pure. It always enhanced his desire to dirty her pure mind . . . .

*****

Monday, the day Jonathan was looking forward to, came— but he was frustrated because he was running late. That was also his fault; last night was a long and passionate one for the married couple. Nevertheless, he made it to the meeting place at the right time. It was a luxurious restaurant, fully furnished with modern technology and design. The restaurant served the best food in town. *As expected, Mr. Hale's choices are always out-of-the-box*, he thought, shaking his head.

"Reservations under Mr. Hale, please," Jonathan said to the hostess standing at the entrance, greeting the customers.

The hostess searched for the name on her iPad, and, when she finally found it, she said, "Come with me, sir. I'll escort you to the table."

Jonathan followed the hostess to a secluded table in the VIP section, where he saw Mr. Hale leaning back on his chair, with his eyes closed.

"Here you are, sir." The hostess's voice caused Mr. Hale to open his eyes and smile brightly when he saw Jonathan standing in front of him. "Your waiter will be here in a few minutes."

Jonathan thanked him and took a seat across from Mr. Hale.

"Hello, sir."

"Hello, young man! How are you doing today?"

"I'm good, sir. I hope I didn't make you wait long."

"No, no. Don't worry; it wasn't a big deal."

"Thank you."

Jonathan let out a sigh of relief.

Both of them conversed for a long time. When the waiter came, they placed their order and resumed the conversation again. Mr. Hale was happy to find himself in Jonathan, and he knew that Jonathan needed to know the truth, sooner or later. The sooner it was out, the better it would be for him.

"Hmm . . . I get what you're saying, young man. It's a little bit tricky what you're asking for, but I guess if we plan it out well, we could achieve it."

"That's why I need your assistance, Mr. Hale. I don't think I can do it alone. I need a powerful backup to destroy the governor and get the senate seat."

"Alright, I'll help you, but . . . ."

"But?"

"You hear me out first. There's a dark secret about your birth that your mother was hiding from you."

"What?" Jonathan was shocked. "What do you mean by that?"

"Jonathan, my son, Lee is not your father. Your mother and I had an affair, and you were born from our love. Your mother kept it hidden from your family because she didn't want to jeopardize her position. Years ago, our families were neighbors, and that's when the affair started. After you were born, Lee found out but never said anything to anyone. He knew

I was sleeping with your mother, even after you were born. I guess you were too young to remember, but my son Duncan would come over and play with you and your brothers."

A cold shiver went down his body, and Jonathan froze like a statue. He knew exactly who Duncan was—the guy who molested Jonathan when they were kids. It all came rushing back.

Does Mr. Hale know what his son did to me? Jonathan thought to himself. *My mother knew, but does he?*

"Where's Duncan now?" Jonathan asked Mr. Hale.

"When he was in his teens, I sent him to boarding school, and we were never really close after that," Mr. Hale told him.

"I haven't seen him in years." Mr. Hale said, taking a sip from his drink.

Now Jonathan could understand Lee's indifferent behavior toward him whenever Jonathan asked about why he didn't receive Lee's love as his other siblings did. Now he knew the answer.

"Why are you telling me this now?" Jonathan asked.

"I need an heir for my business; as you can see, I'm getting old now, and, as I said, I don't have a relationship with my son; somebody

151

needs to take over after me," Mr. Hale said. "Son, I know there are a million questions running in your mind, and I promise to answer every one of them."

"Alright."

"So do we have a deal now?"

Despite all of this new information, Jonathan said, "Yes, I will take over the business!"

*****

Disturbed by the revelations, Jonathan rushed home. He couldn't fathom why his mother had hidden his birth father's identity. His mind was going blank from all the what-ifs. All this time, he had craved his father's attention, never understanding why Lee didn't favor him, why he neglected him, unlike his other siblings. Jonathan remembered how he used to cry in his sleep, asking God what he did wrong.

Jonathan recalled the day he was molested by Duncan. His mother was furious when she walked in and saw what Duncan was doing to him. At that moment, Jonathan realized he was being raped by his half-brother. He knew he never saw Duncan again after that day, but he didn't know why.

Did my mother make Mr. Hale send Duncan away? He thought.

Ellie covered that incident up as if it had never occurred, not only because she was worried, he'd be harassed but also because it could ruin her reputation.

*****

Jonathan knew Mr. Hale had to know what Duncan did to him as a child, but he didn't care. He needed Mr. Hale to help him become a US senator. In the following years, the father and son duo worked hard to take down the governor; they devised a plan for it. Jonathan told Suzanne the truth about his birth, but not about Duncan. Eventhough he knew she'd be the only one standing beside him in difficult and sorrowful times he was too embrarrassed to tell her.

People had noticed Jonathan acting a lot like his mother; his family and friends told him so. His siblings were afraid Jonathan would start behaving as their mother did before she died. Slowly, they all started to distance themselves from him, meeting and talking to him when it was only necessary.

Jonathan didn't mind the distance; he was more focused on naming himself as the next senator and preparing himself to take over his biological father's business. Jonathan's stubbornness and determination pushed him to accomplish his goals. He was finally going to win his mother's seat, or was he?

Chapter 9 – November 5th

No one would've guessed it would all go down that day—the day that proved to be ill-fated to their mother also turned out to be unfortunate for them.

November 5th was the day that tore apart the Peak Family. It was supposed to be a typical day; every family member was looking forward to attending the election night watch party for Jonathan. None of them knew that their lives would change forever that very day. It was like a domino effect; the lives of every member of the Peak family was going to change one by one. Was it a coincidence? It all happened exactly six years after Ellie died.

Lee

Lee was late for Jonathan's election night watch party; it was around six when he finally got home. His instincts were telling him something was horribly wrong, but he kept ignoring them. He just wanted to get home to Holly.

I'm blessed to have a partner in Holly; she's the best thing that has ever happened to me! Lee thought, smiling.

While making his way home, Lee stopped at the bakery shop his wife loved. He wanted to surprise her with a token of his love and searched for some baked goods she'd like. When he finally found one, he asked the person behind the counter to help him. Lee proceeded to give him his credit card to pay for the items.

"Uh . . . sir." The clerk paused. "Your card keeps getting declined."

"What?" Lee said, surprised. "But how could that be?"

"I don't know, sir."

"Can you please try it one more time?"

"Alright." The clerk tried it once again, and the same error was displayed. Lee was puzzled; he couldn't understand how this could've happened. "Sir, do you have any other means to pay for the items?"

"Huh, wait." Lee probed his coat and pants pocket to see if he had any cash with him and found a twenty-dollar bill. "Here."

Exiting the bakery, Lee's mind was still stuck on the fact that his card was rejected. *What a fun event; Holly will surely love this mishap*, Lee thought, chuckling.

"Holly! I'm home!" Lee called out to his wife, stepping his foot inside the house, but no voice could be heard from inside. Lee didn't think much of it and placed the bakery goods in the kitchen. *She must be sleeping.*

"Babe!" He trudged his way to the first floor to their bedroom. Lee pushed the door open, grinning and hoping to catch her off-guard, but it was his turn to be shocked. He glanced around the room; the bed was made, everything was exactly as he'd left it early in the morning, but there was no sign of Holly.

Lee's heart started beating faster, sweat trickling down his forehead and his hands trembling excessively.

He searched the closet: empty.

Her toiletries in the bathroom: gone.

The gifts he bought for her: gone.

Her belongings had all disappeared; it was as if they hadn't been there from the beginning.

He tried to call Holly's number again and again. "The number you are dialing is not in service."

What's going on! Did something happen to her?

Lee called Holly's friends, one by one, but was not able to get a single clue about her whereabouts. He searched for her in the house; he tried to call his children, but none of them answered.

A thought occurred in his mind; Lee knew he wasn't thinking straight, but he had to confirm it to satisfy his inner voice. He slowly and hesitatingly checked his bank account and safe. Just, at that moment, his accountant called him and told him he was just informed Holly used the power of attorney Lee gave her, took all his money, and sold his house. Lee's heart stopped when he learned he was left with no money; he was left broke and homeless. Unable to digest Holly's betrayal, Lee suffered a stroke.

*****

While standing in line at the airport, waiting to leave the country with Chris and all of Lee's money, Holly thought about how much she really did care for Lee and how much she enjoyed being a part of the Peak family. She felt guilty for what she was doing to Lee, but there was a mental hold Chris had on her. She couldn't resist Chris and would do whatever he asked of her. Not only was she struggling with what she did to Lee, but she was also trying to figure out the right time to tell Chris she was pregnant, and she didn't know if the baby was Lee's or his.

Haley

Although it had been years since Haley had seen Christian there were days, she would think about him and get very nervous, and this was one of those days.

Seven thirty-four. Seven thirty-five. Seven thirty-six. Seven-thirty—

"Haley!" Ross was frustrated, watching his wife glance at the clock every second. Haley jumped at his loud call, anxious and scared. "Stop watching it; we'll be at the party on time."

"I know, but . . . ." She paused. "What if he . . . ."

"He won't harm you anymore, darling." Ross embraced her in his arms from behind. " We have talked about this before, I've put a restraining order on him. He'll be behind bars if he tries to come near you."

"Thank you . . . ." She paused and turned her face toward her husband. "Thank you for everything, Ross. If you hadn't forgiven me, I don't know what I would've done. I'm sorry for betraying you—"

"Shh . . . ." He interrupted her and kissed her on her forehead. "It's all in the past, darling. Forget about that now, and let's just focus on our future."

Haley nodded and kissed him, expressing her emotions and thankfulness in that kiss. Ross leaned back from the kiss and teased her. "Now, now. Wasn't someone getting paranoid they wouldn't reach the venue on time?"

"I'm sure Jonathan can wait for us . . . ." She hinted, playful.

Ross chuckled and allowed her to unbutton his shirt, groaning when she placed kisses on his chest along the way. Haley wanted to pour out every ounce of gratitude she had for him; she was unable to understand how she'd cheated on a kind and honest man like Ross.

She sometimes wondered what would've happened if Ross hadn't forgiven her. Who would've stood beside her in this fucked-up situation? Haley knew she didn't deserve Ross, but he always convinced her she was the only one in his heart—now and forever. Haley promised herself she'd amend her mistakes and take care of her family as she was supposed to.

"Babe," Ross murmured, watching his wife lying in his arms, sweat glistening on her nude body. She was glowing, smiling radiantly, and Ross was so awed by her beauty that he forgot what he was about to ask her.

"Mhm . . ." Haley glanced up at her husband, questioning him with her eyes. She blushed furiously when she saw he was mesmerized with her. "Ross? You were saying?" She tried again.

"Oh, yes!" He came out of his daydream and stared at Haley, frowning. "I don't want to, but I think we should go now because, if we don't move now, I don't think I'll let you go afterward."

They both laughed at his cheesy line and hastily dressed up again to attend the watch party. The couple was full of smiles; it was as if they'd found a new way of loving each other. In the midst of it, Haley realized their love didn't die; it only became stronger!

*****

Haley felt a gaze on her as soon as she stepped out of the car. Frightened, she'd been looking over her shoulder for years, but, for some reason, she felt Christian was watching her. She scanned the crowded parking lot but couldn't find the reason behind it.

"Haley!"

Surprised, she turned toward Ross. Seeing him, she relaxed immediately. "What's wrong? You've gone pale, darling."

"Nothing . . . I was just . . . ." She trailed off and shook her head to remove those disturbing thoughts. "Let's go. The kids must be waiting for us."

Ross nodded and stretched out his arm to her. Smiling, she looped her arm through his and paced forward. *It must've been my imagination; I shouldn't be worried about him anymore! Ross said he'd protect me; I believe in him. Nothing could go wrong—*

At that moment, Christian ran up to Haley . . .

Bang! A gunshot.

Haley's beaming face froze, her eyes became enlarged and soulless, and her mouth remained open mid-smile. Hot blood trickled down her forehead to her face and then her black dress.

Bang! Another gunshot.

Christian ran off.

Beside her, Ross fell into a panic, crying desperately for her; he fell down on the ground with her in his arms. He wanted to undo the incident somehow, but the damage was done—two bullets were engraved in her forehead.

A crowd started to gather around the couple, some taking pity on them. In the distance, away from the crowd, a guy dressed in all black was hiding in an alleyway. His hand clenched around a revolver in pure fury and excitement.

I told you, Hal, till death do us part; with that thought, Christian jumped in his car and drove away.

Nancy

It had been years since Nancy raised her hand to Jade. Jade felt closer to Nancy than ever before. The couple had been married for over a year, and Jade felt safe with Nancy, even though she knew Nancy had a violent side. Jade was looking forward to going to the watch party with Nancy.

It was five in the morning when Nancy joined Jade in the shower. The steam from the hot water was making the clear glass door transparent. Nancy hugged Jade from behind, roaming her hands across her body.

"Nancy, I'm really tired," Jade said. "I didn't sleep a wink last night."

"Please." Nancy requested, tenderly kissing her on the shoulder. "I promise this'll be the last time we make love this morning."

"Mhm . . ." Jade moaned, shaking her head.

"I'll make sure you love every minute of our lovemaking." She began placing steamy kisses on Jade's back. "Just give me this, and I'll let you go to the café."

"Alright," Jade told her, panting. The hot water was dripping down their bodies, and Nancy's hand, which was dangerously close to Jade's vagina inclined her to give in.

Nancy made Jade lean on the glass door, arms tightly wrapped around each other, their hands exploring and feeling the other, covered in sweat. The steamy water mixed with their sweet lovemaking, creating a sensual atmosphere in the small glass partition.

The couple had been making love since last night, but it still wasn't enough for Nancy. She didn't want to part from Jade anytime now. Nancy had previously asked her to stay at home, but Jade knew she couldn't stay. It was already getting late; the customers must be waiting outside her cafe now.

I thought it would only take a few minutes, Jade thought, drying her hair. *But it took us two hours!* She shook her head. *Wasn't the shower enough? Why do we have to do it again on the bed?* She groaned. *I guess I underestimated Nancy; her stamina is much greater than I thought.*

Unwinding the towel from her body, Jade started dressing up in a white round-neck T-shirt and striped blue jeans. It was her favorite got-to-go clothes. Zipping her jeans, she peered around the room. *Where did Nancy go?* She thought. *She was here a minute ago; did she already leave?*

"Jade?" Nancy called from downstairs. *Oh, there she is!* Jade shook her head, chuckling.

"Yes?" Jade answered. Collecting her bag, phone, and car keys, she went to find Nancy.

Nancy was in the backyard, sitting on the wooden bench placed on the patio. She was toying with a black box in her hand, moving it back and forth in her hands. Jade was confused; she hadn't seen the box with Nancy last night, nor did she tell her about it. So where did it come from?

"Hey," Jade muttered, walking to the patio and taking a seat beside Nancy.

"Hello, love," Nancy said, kissing her.

165

"Where did you go?" Jade asked. "I thought you left. I was worried, as you were here one minute and the other you weren't."

"Don't worry, love; I'll never leave you." Nancy giggled. "I promise."

Jade smiled, but an uneasy feeling filled her heart. *Why did it seem more like a threat rather than an oath?* Jade dismissed the negative thought and concentrated on what Nancy was telling her.

"So . . . ." Nancy trailed, teasing Jade. "I have a surprise for my sweetheart."

"Really?" Jade asked, excited. "What is it?"

"I think I don't want to tell you now. Hmm, maybe some other day."

"Nancy!"

"Okay, okay." Nancy snickered and passed the black square box to her.

"What's inside it?"

"Stop talking and just open it."

Jade ran her hand on the velvety texture of the box; she'd always loved how smooth rich velvet felt on her skin. She wanted to carefully admire the pattern on the box, but beside her, Nancy was getting impatient.

"Oh My God, Nancy!" Jade gushed, gazing inside the box. "This is so beautiful!"

A beautiful antique rose-cut diamond necklace set was inside the box. It was exactly what Jade had dreamed of for a long time, and Nancy had somehow fulfilled her dream.

"Thank you so much, Cy," Jade said.

"Anything for you, babe," Nancy said.

"Where did you get it from? And when did you buy it? Was it expensive?"

"One question at a time."

"Alright," Jade said, calming herself down. "Where did you get it from?"

"A friend of Haley is a jewelry designer, and I asked her if she could show me a necklace that would be suitable for you."

"Then when did you buy it?"

"Yesterday." Looking at her puzzled expressions, Nancy explained. "It was when I told you I have a business meeting to attend. And, before you ask, it wasn't that expensive."

Jade nodded and leaned back toward Nancy.

"Can I wear it to the party tonight?"

"Of course!" Nancy said excitedly

*****

"Jade."

"Jade!"

"Jade!"

As soon as she heard the tone in Nancy's voice, she knew what was about to come. She hadn't heard that tone in years . . . .

Nancy repeatedly shouted, growing more aggressive and irritated each second by Jade's lack of response. "Where the hell is that woman?" she muttered to herself.

"Jade!" She marched toward the second floor, smashing and destroying everything in her way. "Don't let me find you, babe, or you know what I'll do!"

Slamming the master bedroom door, Nancy glowered around the room and closed the door. She was about to go down when she heard weeping noises coming from the bathroom, down the corridor. *Oh! So there you are, hiding!* She thought, snickering.

Nancy's dominant behavior had returned for no reason on this day; this was the side of Nancy that loved to torment and play sick mind games with Jade. She slightly pushed open the bathroom door, and she knew it would only put more stress on Jade.

Sliding inside, Nancy saw Jade sitting in a corner. Her legs were pushed toward her chest and her arms tightly wrapped around them. Nancy got a sick sense of pleasure seeing her crying. She enjoyed watching the tears flow from Jade's eyes when her eyes followed the wet path from her face to her neck.

Fed up from the cat and mouse game, Nancy shouted, "Jade!"

Jade jumped in the air and paled, hearing Nancy's voice so close to her. Jade didn't know when she came inside the bathroom. "N-N-N-Nancy . . . ."

"Yes, darling, Nancy," Nancy said in a fake sweet voice. "Do you know how long I've been calling you?" Her eyes turned dark. "Do you think you can ignore me?"

Before Jade could blink, Nancy stretched her arm and grabbed her by the hair, pulling her, all the way to the first floor where she usually gave Jade her punishments.

Nancy shoved her to the floor and emptied all her rage on her, kicking, punching, and slapping her. "I told you!" Nancy shouted. "I told you, didn't I? If only you'd listened, I wouldn't have to do this to you!" Her voice got louder and louder with every statement. "This is all your fault! Everything is your fault! I don't understand why you make me do this to you!"

Jade's white summer dress was now red, bathed in blood. Her face was swelling; there was no way anyone would be able to recognize her if they saw her. Nancy leaned back and admired her artwork, grinning in a twisted way, "You look beautiful in red, Jade."

"P-p-p-l-e-a-s-s-e . . . lea-a-ave . . . m-m-me . . ." Jade cried out.

"Leave you? How can I leave you, love? This is the time to prove your love to me!"

"No! Anything but that . . . please."

Nancy disregarded her pleas and began to undress her. "See! This is your fate! Remember no one will save you from me. You'll always belong to me; you're my wife!"

Nancy was so enraged she didn't realize she pushed and kicked Jade so much they'd spilled outside the house. One of the neighbors saw Nancy beating Jade and called the police. Nancy didn't hear the sirens and only stopped when three officers yelled.

"Hands up! You're under arrest!" The first officer handcuffed her.

Two officers dragged the squirming and screaming Nancy to the police car. Nancy was infuriated; she was shouting incoherent words to the police. When the police were unable to control her, they tased her.

The other officer, with the help of Jade's neighbor, took Jade to the hospital. The doctors conveyed that her condition was serious; she was beaten so severely she was admitted to ICU with a broken arm and a collapsed lung.

Trinity

It had been a year since the last time Kristen encountered Trinity. She'd become busy with other investigations, not having time for anything other than her work.

Kristen was an undercover name that she used to get close to Trinity; her real name was Emily. She and her brother worked as undercover FBI agents. However, she never stopped thinking about Trinity, about what and how he was doing.

"What are you thinking?" Seth asked her one day.

"No, I didn't," she told him, absentminded. Seth chuckled. Emily glanced at him and asked, "Why are you laughing?"

"I'm laughing at how love-sick you've become." He teased.

"What are you even talking about? Why would I be love-sick? There's no way I could love anyone like Trinity Peak." She huffed.

"I didn't say his name!" He smirked, looking at her sister. Not only were they twins but also best friends. Seth would know Emily's feelings without her talking about them.

"Uh," she stammered, flustered. "I . . . umm . . . I guessed. I didn't mean him to be exact, you know."

"Whatever helps you sleep at night, Em." Seth dodged the empty box of cereal and ran out of the house before Emily could throw anything else.

Ring. Ring.

Who's calling me? She thought. *This is the phone I use when I'm undercover! Gosh! They can be so persistent!* Emily picked up her phone to look at who was calling.

Trinity.

"What!?" she shouted, her voice vibrating in the empty house. "Why's he calling me now? When I left his place that day, my part of the investigation was done! Did he find out who I really am?" She mumbled.

Hesitating, Emily picked up the call and said, "Hello?"

"Hey, Kristen!" Trinity's deep voice greeted her; she closed her eyes and savored the moment. "How are you, beautiful?"

"Trinity! I'm alright. How are you faring without me?"

"Not good, babe. Not good. I'm standing on the terrace, ready to jump down." He joked.

"Stop overacting, Trinity." She rolled her eyes.

"I missed your voice," Trinity suddenly said.

"W-what?" Emily said, startled.

"Don't be so shocked, babe. I can be a loveable person too. But anyway, I literally did miss you," he said. "Can we meet?"

"Trinity . . . I don't know . . . ." she faltered.

"My baby brother is running for my mother's senate seat, and we're having a watch party tonight. I wanted to officially invite you to the watch party and introduce you to my family."

"Uh . . . I don't know if it's a good idea right now."

"Please? Just this once." He pleaded. "How about we go out after the party?"

"Okay," she said, giving in to his persistence.

"Thank you!" he exclaimed. "Let's meet at seven. I'll have my driver pick you up when you get here."

"Alright. I have to go now, Trinity. I'll meet you at seven."

"I'll be waiting!" Trinity said and hung up. Emily was both terrified and happy; she was meeting him after a year. At that moment, her work phone rang again, but this time, it was her boss.

"Today's the day," he told Emily.

"We want you there when we make the arrest; after all, we could not have built this case without the evidence you uncovered."

Emily didn't want to be a part of Trinity's arrest. She knew the way she got the flash drive was illegal and wouldn't hold up in court if anyone found out. Also, she didn't know why or how, but she had feelings for him.

*****

It was a big day for Trinity; the day he'd been waiting for months was finally here. He was excited to take his company to a higher level. He knew that, after today, his brother would be a US senator, and no one could ever touch him. The FBI would have no choice but to back down from their accusations.

Ring. Ring.

"Hello," he said.

"Trinity, where are you?" Jonathan asked anxiously.

"I'm at the office right now."

"What? What are you doing there? You should be here with me; don't you know how important today is?"

Trinity rolled his eyes at his brother's exaggerations.

"I know. Don't worry, little brother, I'll be there as promised."

"Alright. I'll be waiting for you!"

Trinity chuckled and hung up the call; he wondered how Suzanne tolerated him.

"Please, sir, stop." came a voice from outside his office.

"Get out of my way."

"You cannot go inside without permission."

"I don't need your permission to arrest someone. I have a warrant!"

"Please, stop, sir. Security! Security!"

There was a commotion outside Trinity's office. The voice was getting louder and louder. This type of altercation wasn't a new thing for Trinity; it had been happening for a year now. Every month the FBI would arrive with armed officers and leave when they couldn't find anything.

They should be gone by now; why are they still here fighting this much? He wondered, stroking the wrinkles on his forehead. *Alright! Let's see what they're up to now!*

He buzzed the intercom. "Glenn, ask Sean to come inside with them."

Ten minutes later, his office was surrounded by people; the agents had their guns positioned at him.

"Yes? Can I know why you people are making a commotion inside my company?" Trinity said in a bored tone.

"We have a warrant to arrest you for fraud and money laundering," the agent said.

"Warrant?" He scoffed. "You need to have proof before you can issue a warrant, and, as I know, you people don't have any, right?"

"Wrong!" A female voice corrected him. Glancing at the woman who emerged from the crowd, Trinity's jaw dropped.

"K-Kristen?" Trinity said, horrified.

"No, not Kristen. Emily." She smirked. "Special Agent Emily Martin."

It was like a cold bucket of water had splashed Trinity, paralyzing him for a moment.

Irked, Trinity shouted, "Y-y-you bitch!" He lunged forward to strangle her in a rage but was pulled back by four agents.

"Just you wait! I'll destroy you as soon as I get my hands on you! Nobody can play with Trinity Peak! Nobody!" Trinity kept on threatening and yelling while getting dragged by the agents to the car.

All of the employees that saw him knew this was the end of Trinity Peak.

"Thank you," the special agent in charge said to Emily. "You've done a fantastic job!"

Smiling, Emily said, "I can't wait to see him in an orange prison jumpsuit."

Little did they know, Emily didn't mean that; in her heart, it hurt her to see him in handcuffs.

Dean

Dean was up all night taking Benzos and drinking; he knew it was Jonathan's big day, but he needed drugs and alcohol. The boys were up early, playing and making noise. This was the last straw for Dean. He walked out of his room toward the kitchen with a blank stare. He got a knife out of the drawer and headed to Blake's room. Blake had his headphones on, listening to music. He didn't hear his father open the door. As soon as Dean opened the door, he immediately jumped on Blake and slashed his throat. He walked down the hall to the room where Ray and Peter were playing. On his way there, he passed a picture of Ellie hanging on the wall. He touched her picture, smearing Blake's blood all over her picture. As soon as he saw Ray, he stabbed him in the chest and stomach. Peter was so shocked at what he was seeing, he stood frozen in his place. He looked at his father's eyes and didn't recognize who this man was. Peter was standing in a puddle of his own urine when Dean grabbed him and stabbed him.

It was late when Kat left the hospital; she'd been going to a therapist for a year now. Ever since Dean raped her, her life had turned upside down. She couldn't sleep properly without having nightmares of that night. She felt herself in constant danger now.

When the drug's effect wore off, Dean would try to apologize. But Kat knew it wouldn't do any good.

No matter how many times she scrubbed herself, the dirt wouldn't disappear. It was there on her skin, on every part of her body, visible but unseen. For a long time, Kat felt disgusted by herself; she had been violated by the person she loved the most.

What have I done wrong? Why did my life turn out like this? She thought.

But enough was enough! Kat had decided to move out with her kids and go somewhere far away where Dean couldn't find them. She thought she'd take her kids after the watch party.

The moment Kat pulled into the driveway, she knew something wasn't right. But what? She couldn't put her finger on it. Her instincts were telling her that something was amiss. The kids couldn't stay this silent when they knew she was home; they were notorious for being rowdy boys.

Now she was getting anxious! Kat glanced inside the window, trying to get a clue as to what was wrong. The inside seemed to be normal; it didn't feel like something had gone horribly wrong.

Kat hastily unlocked the door. Her hands were trembling immensely; she was not able to grasp the key properly.

The creaking noise of the door sent shivers down her spine. *What is this eerie feeling?*

"Dean?"

No answer.

"Peter?"

No answer.

"Blake?"

No answer.

"Ray?"

No answer.

Where are they? Are they playing with me?

"Come out, you all! This isn't funny now. We need to get ready for the watch party."

Kat slowly walked toward the children's room, and that's when she saw the blood. Her bag fell from her shoulder to the floor. Kat's eyes widened, her mouth hung open, and her breath stopped. Her eyes took in her children's bodies. The kids were lying down in pools of their own blood, one beside the other. The room was gruesome, blood splattered everywhere. She opened the door to Blake's room and saw him lying with his headphones on, the music still playing.

Kat broke down, seeing her children stabbed; she had no doubt Dean did this to them. Her poor kids. *What did they ever do to you, Dean? Why did you do this!* She thought, crying.

181

She didn't know where Dean was. She called the paramedics in a panic, praying that her kids would survive.

When the police arrived, they searched the house and found Dean hanging from a beam in the garage with blood all over his clothes and the knife lying on the floor beneath his feet.

Jonathan

Jonathan kept pacing back and forth; he was starting to get nervous, waiting for his family. It was an important day for him— November 5th, the election day. This day would decide if he was going to win his mother's senate seat or not. *Where are they? Why haven't they come yet? None of my family is here!*

"Calm down, Jon," Suzanne said.

"How can I, Suzanne?" Jonathan grumbled. "The results are about to come in, and no one is here yet. What's more important than this?"

"Maybe they're just running late; cut them some slack, please. They'll be here."

"I hope so."

Suzanne slipped her arms around his shoulders and massaged them lightly to help him reduce some tension. Jonathan was a controlling and demanding husband, but Suzanne could tell that he loved her way more than anyone else.

"Thank you." Jonathan turned around and kissed her softly on the lips.

"That's what I'm here for." She winked at him, joking, making Jonathan laugh loudly. He needed this.

"I love you, darling." He confessed, kissing her again.

"I love you too, Jonathan." She kissed him back.

At that moment, Jonathan's phone rang. He didn't recognize the number but thought it was one of his siblings.

"Hello"

"Hello, Jonathan, this is Duncan"

"Who?"

"Duncan Hale. Remember me?"

"Yes, I remember you! How did you get this number, and why the hell are you calling me?!"

"Our father gave me your number."

"So, you know!" Jonathan said in an aggravated tone.

"Yes, I know now; that's why our father and your mother sent me away," Duncan said humbly.

"What do you want? I am extremely busy!"

"First, I want to congratulate you on all your success, and I know you'll be a great senator . . . Jonathan, I want to apologize for the things I did to you when we were kids. I have cancer; I don't have much time left to live, and I needed to tell you this. I know you may not forgive me, but I want to say I'm sorry."

"You're right; I don't forgive you, and you can rot in hell!" Jonathan hung up his phone and tossed it on the desk.

An hour passed, and the results began coming in. Jonathan was upset. Although there was a large crowd of supporters in the hotel ballroom downstairs, besides Suzanne, his daughters, and Mr. Hale, none of his family were there to support him. Nevertheless, he let it go, as he needed to concentrate on the results and possible victory speech.

Jonathan didn't mention to Mr. Hale that Duncan called him. Their eyes were fixated on the television, restless and uneasy, waiting for the news that would hopefully bring them immense joy. Albert, Jonathan's campaign manager, entered the room and said, "Sir, I have some horrible news about your family!"

"What is it?!" Jonathan said while still watching the television.

At that moment, the news reporter announced:

"Jonathan Peak has won his first term as a US senator!"

THE END

About the Author

Kyle Washington is an intuitive writer who scripts ravishing stories that keep his readers wanting more. Page after page, his stories lead to exciting scenarios, and readers can't put his writings down. He is devoted to his family and is an avid reader, versatile writer, and lover of art and literature.

He is originally from Houston, Texas, and is the youngest of 5 children. He raised his daughters as a single father while working as an executive for a major corporation.

He enjoys traveling the world meeting new people and asking to hear their stories. *Empty Calories* is his debut novel and was inspired by the people he has met throughout his life.

Made in the USA
Middletown, DE
10 March 2023

26527661R00109